STAB FRENZY

STAB FRENZY

~~FIRST ON VENUS~~
~~INSTALLATION VIEW~~
~~TILL DRESDEN~~
~~DEEP FAKE~~
~~TRANSFORMERS~~
~~ART HORROR~~
~~ROTTEN PINOCCHIOS~~

~~a novel~~

GARY J. SHIPLEY

Apocalypse Party

Cover Design by Gary J. Shipley
Typesetting by Mike Corrao

Cover Art: Paul Thek, *Untitled* (Meat Piece with Flies), 1965.

Paperback: 978-1-954899-20-9

Excerpts have been featured in *SELFFUCK*, *Fanzine*, Action Books Strange Fiction Series, and *HARSH*, in *Mutations* (Infinity Land Press), and the following anthologies: *Stories of the Eye* (Weirdpunk Books), *Children of the New Flesh: The Early Work and Pervasive Influence of David Cronenberg* (11:11 Press), and *Infinity Land Press Anthology* (Infinity Land Press).

I need a new way to write my name.

—Douglas A. Martin

Keep writing those confessional poems
In the voice of a narco-terrorist
Or drawing cute pictures of dinky murder scenes.
But at least admit that art is a crime
And you're a criminal, and start expecting
To get caught, just when you least expect it.

—Jim Gustafson

Above all, artists are people who want to
become inhuman.

—Apollinaire

CONTENTS

A SAD THING
ABOUT ASYLUMS

MY ACTIVITIES WERE SUPPOSEDLY VAGUE. THEY'VE got me down as a businessman, a lowly salesman, a failing one, debts racking up, suicide looming, only it wasn't that. If they could see me listening to Bach with all the lights turned off…, then they'd realize how well I am, how I shirk regret for a living, how refined I look in the dark.

She was getting older, they all were. But she was less pretty in a way that goaded my investment. Had the neck turned suddenly scraggy that way? Had the skin around the eyes turned that shade of bruised apples overnight? There must have been some irreconcilable asymmetry. But all this is ingrowing toenails when I've already amputated the foot. Such an adorable confusion when Thomas was young and adamant about how the sparrows in our garden had given him the flu. My face quivering like it might cry, feeling disfigured – like when I had work done in Eastern Europe (for some since abandoned project referencing Kōbō Abe and the material undoing of identity) and the expressions I couldn't make were unlicensed versions of the ones I saw on the nurses from my bed.

3

I took the baby teeth with me when I left. The oval 18th-century gold and tortoiseshell trinket box was co-incidental. First and foremost, I wanted my children's molars. I was proud, I suppose, that their teeth had fallen out. That they'd lived that long and further, with less-soft teeth than before and the childish fats all gone. After the rain, no senility would come. Timeless now, like the ancients, like the secrecies of Jesus. It must have been an odd sensation when the bullets went in; but over so quickly, the alteration kind of cosmetic, the time left around it numbed – barely a murmur, the tinge of some fading conceit. Me stood there, composure of a saint, and more dangerous than I looked. *Coming with the daffodils and dying with the roses.*

For the foreignness of someone like me, it's not enough to just get born one place and end up somewhere else – although I've done that too. Mine's a forensic al-terity, my difference multiple explosions. I'm strip-lit clouds, awake in glimpses, incidentally human. To get this way I evaporate and materialise. And finding I could do it, I didn't stop until I was out of breath, unstable, somewhere in between myself and becoming slowly done for. Returning to the thing I did, I go missing. I catch sight of my no longer being here. Nothing disturbs me, not even the pulse of the house.

Open heart surgery on a boat across the Med, from moorings off Fréjus to a port in Corsica, then on to North Africa, losing blood every minute, sobbing with vomit. I think maybe I hid out in a forest in Bagnols-en-Forêt for close to a year before going anywhere. I think I remember being surrounded by trees, and eating rabbits trapped by their feet with wire and, when there was nothing else, repulsively muscular grubs.

Everything in moderation didn't sit well with my vanities. And all my angles are unspecified, all explanations vulgar. Did you see how gorgeous the world was when you looked up into the downpour? Did you see how comingled we were in our simultaneous fairy tales? We crawled out of the burning animals alive. And that's something to hold on to, now our similitude's gone limp.

It's different: I wage love, you absorb hate. I never called the scars up your arms baroque, but here comes the invective anyway. It's not true: our combined imbalance won't even us out. I only wanted to meditate on extinction until the sky changed colour forever. I only wanted to deepfake my own face into this new life.

An underfed horse drinking from the baptistery between your legs. I don't have to understand mental trauma for it to reimagine who I am. Again with the *Call of Duty* all day and no sunlight. Again with passively excreting this frantic immobility. Again with the language of squirrels as we chew up our nails.

I forgot about the diary I didn't keep. And all the pages inside listing all my non-events, in artificial cubicles, in my testimony of just how slowly I can suffocate if I try. I only wanted to remember why it was I never wrote it down. Something about the ritual humiliation of a residential area, a wolf circling in small rooms and the dismal composition of its scent. The ignominy of a monster made to smile and be polite as if dipped into by a whole family at once. Anxious pen marks striated on my thoughts instead. The diary I didn't keep lists how many separate instances of neglect it took, lists the crisis broken up into minutes, the little injuries that groomed me for a life lived between the eyebrows of everyone I met. I picked something up along the way. I went on as if my facial hair was the 51st state of America. As if my alienation had been sanctioned from the very top. Harboured by the 1% to contaminate the 99. The chosen fugitive of all invisible elites.

Given the choice, I'd condense every conspiracy theory into a single theory. I'd insist it be taught in classes in prisons for the criminally insane. Speculating on my whereabouts would be mandatory. Any talk of deflationist theories of truth would get you the chair.

So don't come to my bunker for anything less than oblivion. Don't pretend your time spent in a federal jail in Manhattan qualifies you to rank the relative awfulness of my crimes, like they are isomorphic to your frames of reference, like you can lance my conscience with your fingernails. I've tried to stay urbane throughout all this, but I can't see where I'm going. It's like the future's just symbolism for your being joyless, and nobody will ever arrive to carry my luggage.

My hands in your filthy hair, squeezing. You can watch me while I do it. Your swallow-tail tongue can hold my cigarette.

POSTFACE
PREFACE

PLEASE NOW, AT LAST, AT LEAST, A FUCKING END TO this. Or failing that, I'll find out how far I can go before it's too late; I'll unearth the deepest, darkest inanity beyond even this super-silliness of being human. I've sacrificed my family for this chance, there has to be something. And the things he did, he can hardly think of them now. Things we all do, after all, all of them: so many subliminal hagiographies of shit.

As a prolusory distraction, I was wondering about Xavier's whereabouts and how you'd go about fashioning an escape from something like that. I surmised someone fickle and vain would stop there (attention all over the place and none of it properly itemised), and maybe I thought I could blame it on him. And there was always the option of doing Xavier and the House of Terror properly, but people bore me so quickly. I found the case intriguing enough as a starting point for something else; I find that with most things. Whatever I create has to justify itself, and the details of a human life are never enough. Humans are mostly dull as dry pebbles; and even when on

odd occasion they exceed my expectations, it isn't nearly
enough on its own. All those oh-so-human stories and
their myriad interactions, each one done to death already,
bore the absolute living shit. I don't care, I'm not interested, give me something else. These supposedly nuanced,
supposedly revelatory, profound, important, forensic, or
whatever, confections are all of them stratospherically uninspired and unimportant regurgitations of the same one
human blandness. Your human life is nothing. Is nobody
else this searingly incurious? It can't just be me.

I couldn't bring myself to write around the art we
made, so I'm writing through it instead – through the
nasty, sallow guts of it. It's better this way. You'll get a
feel for what it is to grow out of feeling anything. And if
you don't, I don't care.

In the first sentence of *Galaxies*, Barry N. Malz-
berg wrote the following disclaimer: "this will not be a
novel so much as a series of notes toward one." It was,
of course, a novel, and a superlative one, a novel more
impressive than many others laying claim to the classi-
fication. And once more with the futile quitclaim comes
Henry Miller, in *Tropic of Cancer*, writing "This then?
This is not a book." So all in all, seems these works, like
us, find it difficult to disown themselves. This thing,
however, whatever it is, really is less a novel, less a book,
and more a foaming at the mouth. Whatever it is it is
something, at least that, not nothing, and imperfect like
a faded bruise. Truthfully, I hope it isn't a novel; I hate
most novels – relationshippy lumps of saccharine gloop,
so poignant, so awful, prose like a granny's armpit sweat,
all the people being so very people-like (*oh isn't it so like*

us, so very very clever how they hold the mirror like that),
the de minimis propinquities of a dull mammalian order
repeated over and over till they make you sick – and have
no desire to add to their number. This said, I'll resume:

We are First on Venus, we are Rotten Pinocchios, we are
Till Dresden, we are Transformers. Whoever we are we're
going to make you all pay for what you've done, for what
you are and what you've made us do. We wouldn't even be
here if it wasn't for you, and so this retribution, and so this
scraping of fingernails across the surface of your brains.

When we met again in Dresden we'd be divested
of our identities, or that was the idea. I would be equal
parts Xavier, some disgusting mash-up of runaway selfhood equating in the end to no self at all; Gogo would
be corroded by the poor-taste-joke-gone-bad of art-sex,
more liver rot and dried noodles than African-shame-
boi-fresher tearing out New School hearts so easy it
hurt; and Uta criminalised within an inch of herself, so
smeared in genocider plasma and speciesist protestations,
so exorcised of so much hate her DNA is crumbling; and
lastly Gerhard, just all the movies, all the locations and
reenactments, all streaming image and impersonalized
vision. And we would come together, the four ciphers,
in that Dresden hotel room and gestate the anti-miracle,
the faceless volte-face.

As a counterpoint to current trends we advocate
an Alien Art, an art removed from any known human
identity: art from the gulf, if you will – art from the
cosmic indifference of the universe without us. If art,
as Arthur C. Danto claims, is "embodied meaning," we

set out to if not break then bend this definition all out of recognizable shape. We would make art from disembodied meaning, and from embodied non-meaning, we would make art from its own unmaking, a wakeful nightmare from a dream of art. And this would be true Art Horror, absorbing your every effort to invest it with meaning, your increasingly desperate projections, giving you nothing in return.

I am one quarter the collective, whose job it is to not only document this new art (our rancid cavity) but present it here, in the thing you are reading. It falls on me the way buildings do when oversleeping, with the same inevitability. But keeping in mind how it's in some people's interest not to have a shared language (*how can I possibly be this special if I allow myself to be understood?*) my only cache is my experiential divergence, my unwavering impenetrability as lubricant, and I'm not sacrificing that for any amount of common ground.

PRELIMINARY
FACESUCK

GERHARD IS IN SEOUL PRETENDING TO KILL WOMEN.

Gogo is selling their body for shots and ramen in a bedsit in St. Pauli, Hamburg.

Uta is everywhere there are farmers of meat or fur thinking how she can best stop them being alive. How she can turn them into piggies or moomoos or mink.

I am in a secret location merging with Xavier Dupont de Ligonnès.

We had seen all the art and what we didn't hate we were so emphatically over. But still art was the only thing we wanted to do, the only occupation both self-consciously silly and potentially catastrophic enough to satiate our cravings. There was poetry, I suppose, but it seems we still retained some small residuum of pride.

We shared a submerged view.

We wanted whatever we did not to be defined by what was done.

We wanted the long sinewy tendrils of art to make us more than we were. We couldn't live with only being alive.

11

We didn't want to fill rooms with inflatables, seeds, sheds, darkness, light, insects, cardboard, furniture, a bouncy castle, a black pillow, a dying horse, balloons, text, Felix the Kolossal Kat, fire, bicycles, hay, carpet, linoleum, tents, teeth, caravans, taxidermy, dioramas, monitors, donuts, beds, mannequins, cars, trains, planes, baths, trees, teddy bears, cameras, feathers, formaldehyde, tyres, tin cans, cabinets, frames, bones, bombs, barbed wire, candy-floss, dead bodies, cigarettes, more rooms, pianos, videos, virtual realities, railings, mazes, toys, skeletons, swings, candles, humans, bricks, terracotta, cooking utensils, shelving, books, sweets, neon, cat litter, smoke, cake, partitions, breeze blocks, prescription meds, mirrors, portraits, polystyrene, rats, cosmetics, fungi, diving boards, cement mixers, foliage, ball bearings, instruments, Perspex, pots and pans, sinks, cages, lasers, boxes, ovens, showers, nails, screws, shells, bunnies, organs, fetuses, ghosts… no reformed lumps of any material: no china, no soil, no rubble, no blood, no oil, no concrete, no elephant shit, no shit, no semen, no piss, no hair, no skin, no rubber, no metal, no stone, no chewing gum, no fabrics, no lard, no lead, no fibreglass, no chocolate, no fruit, no glass, no wood, no leaves, no fingernails, no plastic, no gypsum, no bronze, no spelter, no marble, no mud, no gold, no diamonds, no ice… no fish, no 3D animations, no flowers, no foam, no polluted anything, no images, no nothing, or maybe just nothing, maybe the suck of the void, maybe…

Nothing seemed worth doing but we decided to do it anyway – as prescribed.

We didn't want to copy everything again.

We didn't want to taxonomize light.

We didn't want to spend years painting paint.

We didn't want to sculpt a fucking thing.

We didn't want to appropriate, repurpose or recontextualize anything.

We did not want to be merely reactive, some rebranded kalliphobia uglifying human existence one exhibition catalogue at a time.

We didn't just want to put meat in the Brillo Box, we wanted the Brillo Box to put meat into us – wanted to embody the disembodiment. (First Thek, then Bidlo, was it time to redo Andy's Brillos again?)

We liked Jens Haaning's *Take the Money and Run*, but we didn't want the money: we wanted to take more than that; we wanted to take anything and everything that makes your life worth living and chew it up and shit it out and feed it back to you. And we wanted you to gorge on it without wanting to, to need it without pleasure.

Danto says the end of art arrives when you can't tell the difference between art and reality, saving art from its end at the hands of Duchamp and Warhol by discovering the invisible differences at work in their most challenging pieces. We believe art can only begin when it ends. There is nothing else left. We will show you how.

CRAZY WALLS

THE STIGMA OF BEING A MURDERER ISN'T QUITE THE aphrodisiac they'd have you believe.

All these online reports have me where I'm not. I was spotted in Glasgow but it wasn't me. And just the other day in Chicago, there I was, only I was here. The man spoke with a French accent, so it couldn't have been me: I don't imperil my freedom that way. I don't even quote Baudelaire anymore, or Rimbaud, or the much-maligned Marquis. Who's Sartre? Who's Camus? Who's René Daumal? I pretend Lautrémont was his real name.

I read the Golden State Killer has a micro-penis, and how he was a cop for all those years. And somehow the two things seem to go together, like a micro-penis in the orifices of reluctant women.

I'm thrilled by obsessives, I admire them: their lives so absurd they almost make sense, their futilities less futile in their extremity somehow. Robert Graysmith, Michelle McNamara, Tom Voigt, Paul Haynes, Michael Butterfield... methodical fanatics are like heroic figures to me. I employ their methods in an effort to apprehend myself. The happiness of that much reality, the possibility of an answer, so many plans, a thousand zig-zags, but I fail at being this or that. It's also how I imagine Grigori

Perelman lives, with his mother, but alone as well: the most vibrant and intricately patterned butterfly fluttering about inside a box room in the dark.

My manias, though, must remain pure. They can never go anywhere. They must never arrive. I don't want to solve anything; I don't want to catch a killer. Am *I* not the killer? Do I need anything else? I want to be a character in a Robbe-Grillet novel that when read out loud is the exact duration of my life. In other words, I want my research to fail; I want it to be useless, I want it to be art. My obsession will make little or no progress, and be practiced underground. I'll drown in information, in spurious patterns and intolerable reams of data, glugging till I flop.

Of the things I'm capable of, most aren't even technically possible. Or else I've done them already. And as exciting as it sounds, I'm only locked inside a room to avoid being recognized. And the things I'm destroying weren't disposed to immortality anyway. Could it be I'm not as purely anatomical as I thought, that the edge is not as precipitous as it looks, but more of a slope, and day in day out isn't motionless at all? Tell me, is it still enough, when anonymising, to remove the hands and teeth?

I'm going to make a wall like every obsessive makes a wall, by adorning an already existing wall with all the fragments of my obsession: photographs, pages of highlighted and encircled text, connecting strings, newspaper clippings, maps, timelines, rainbow cork board pins scattered in discursive yet meaningful arrangements. It will be my wall of failure: of the men I didn't apprehend, the prostitutes I never killed, the convicts I never rescued, the banks I never robbed. My wall of disquiet. I'll keep adding to it until I am forced to include adjacent walls. It will spread like a fungal infection. I'll place a viewing seat at some precisely measured distance, where I'll sit for hours studying what I've done (by failing to do anything). There will also be tables with computer monitors, at least three, probably four, similarly sized, playing looped videos of things and people pertinent to the investigation – the investigatory detritus of my non-investigation – to which my eyes will travel when the stillness of the wall becomes oppressive.

On the wall, down by the skirting, is a photograph of Paul McCarthy shitting into his own mouth. There's the big white beard, the cap; I'm sure it's him. I wrote his name on the back. It's there to remind me of something, but I'm not sure what. It will come to me. Sometimes one of the monitors will play snippets of *Painter* or *Experimental Dancer*. I sourced them from UbuWeb and they help to contextualise the seriousness of the wall. Above that same monitor are photos of my family: five separate portraits, five separate smiles – one of them a little off (as if maybe they knew). The see-through pigmentation of our French aristocratic privilege everywhere. Pinned next to them is Lorca's "New York (Office and Denunciation)," where I have underlined the many of those that smash the sky to bits. Some might consider this juxtaposition bad taste, but it's all in keeping with the provocation of the wall itself.

The crazy wall is an extension of the investigation or crime board – often referred to as simply *the board* – and the crazy room an extension of that. I guess, the thing is, I want too much of everything to the point that I settle for less than I started with. I sit in my chair and smoke and look at what I've amassed. I just sit and smoke and think, as if an answer is on the way. As if the answer that arrives won't be a further irritation, another irresolute itch in some inaccessible area of the bodies we're trying so hard to sleep inside. We are mangy in our chairs. I think of it as a kind of theology of moments, a laboratory of furtive howling. I hear myself talking in some unknown dialect. I voice as if from a lurching sea.

The meaning of futility is such a delicate thing. The appetite that consumes itself. The vampiric consumption of my thick French blood. The one question that never goes away: What am I avoiding? Everything a distraction from whatever the answer is, but then the answer's not there. Or it's straightaway lost among the trees, with the forest on fire, with the squirrels turned to charcoal, with my yellowing eyes and skin, my failing liver.

I could be heard developing a belly. Sleeping vertically, suspended by my feet. The irrelevance of a disposition.

I have to get out of here: I'm forgetting the weather. What do I have to do to become intolerable to myself? There was a moment right before I shot one of them, I forget which, when the rifle bullet itself seemed so very precious. Such a weird concentration of emotion in such an inert lump of metal. People will say it's displacement, but they weren't there. No one was. Even I wasn't there, not really.

I sometimes like to imagine I'm holed up in an apartment in some dilapidated project in America. I look at pictures of them and see myself on the other side of one of the windows. I never go out. I have a silly amount of locks and chains on the front door; it would be easier to come in through the walls. I keep pictures of the best ones pinned up in a row: Queensbridge Houses, Robert Taylor Homes, Magnolia Projects, Pruitt-Igoe, Cabrini Gree, Hotel Iveria, Avalon Gardens, and Imperial Courts. If I live there it's because it's too dangerous to go out. I immerse myself in something insanely abstract and esoteric. I live inside whatever it is I'm doing, and barely eat or sleep because of it. Sometimes it's a literary form so intricate and extravagant that nobody has ever come close. Other times it's a philosophical theory so convoluted and arcane that it fills thousands of pages of tiny spidery script and hand drawn diagrams that would take a lifetime for anyone else to decipher. I imagine the same thing contained in just a few lines, the brilliant simplicity of which will belie the decades I spent searching for it. Surpassing the Duchampian revolution in art, this discovery will reconfigure the very fabric of human meaning. It will make it mean something. No one will ever again wonder why it is their senescence feels so vicious.

At a certain time on a certain day, at a train station in Paris, I could see in people's faces how they didn't want to do this anymore. They'd soaked up their lives and were full with every new kind of emptiness. I followed the rules. I refrained from smoking. I didn't talk to anyone. I took my secrets to the grave – the one in Fourqueux, unmarked, posing like nature. I swallowed all the acorns. What was left but waiting? The meditation exercise at the top of my voice. And then nothing. No saplings in sight. Only bad guts and a mutilated tree, and the saplings that refused to grow, because my stomach wasn't soil, wasn't a labyrinth of nutrients, but thin air, the sedimented nothing of my habits.

I glom what life I can from this infinite fatigue. What kind of man prays in every direction at once? I'm clammy to the bone. Let us alone with our technology and our sorrow. Our sorrow without history. Our history prescinded from our insulated state.

BARBARIAN
SUMMER

It's not much to ask: I just want everything to stop. It's about the only thing that keeps me going, and why I'm into the gear all of a sudden. Strictly recreational, mind, and I never inject. It's just my holiday from everything else: think Rachel Ticotin in *Fort Apache, The Bronx*, or Philip Seymour Hoffman in *Before the Devil Knows You're Dead*, or Toni Servillo in *The Consequences of Love*. And I know these touchstones only bode one way, but what doesn't end well does at least end. Anyway, I'm on the foil, it's all good, not like I'm slamming it up a vein in one go, not like I've given up on invoking all the strangers I might become.

My crimes were only crimes if you think that by surviving you're escaping something. As I always say, if you're not squinting at the daylight you're not properly awake. I'm exaggerating: I mean… like I always say anything. I was left too long is all, and now I'm overflowing and fervid and this sleeplessness is turning into a kind of sleep. I have the constant feeling that I'm due to arrive somewhere else, and the impossibility of such a place.

The sky every third day looking like mud. It's a pattern I've observed and I'm sticking to it. If we come apart that's that. I'm trying to be as erratic as possible, so I won't be followed. Being this person over time is the one disguise I can't bring myself to relinquish. I could count myself differently, but what would be the point?

Afterwards, I washed entire landscapes from my hands, whole topographies of planning. I concede that my own personal horrors are trivial compared to some, but the concession is emptier every time. When I hurt I hurt more than the history of the entire world's hurt. I can't change that. I only need other people to exist so I can shrink my pain. What I did, I did because it was the only thing left, and now I'm the only thing left. A thing like me, the vilest of the vile: I read what they say.

An odd sensation between my eyes, like someone has their finger pressed there. I get the taste of metal, the smell of drains. The sucking sounds of sexual parts is not something I've ever confused for tenderness. I know the differences between things, even the imperceptible ones. They found her body in the basement one warm evening in summer. Only partly concealed: a leg, just the calf and the foot, the piss of a passing cat splashed up between the neatly manicured toes. Around the same time there's a picture of me slobbering from all the tranquilizers I was taking. I have a watered-down sense of who I was back then. A glib little angel converging on every romanticised notion I had of what exorcising my humanity might mean. Oh I was the worst. Really, the absolute worst. You see, it's hard to resemble anything other than what you are, and harder still to resemble that.

I'm taking liberties with your patience already, I can feel it. These rhapsodies, though, are sneaking and decorous and unprepared for third-party scrutiny. They're almost Rilkean in their inexpressibility, but I'll get there. You can blame me. Who else is coming close?

As well as all the other things, I'm the best and the worst kind of snob. In other words, I can hide my contempt in the most extravagant kindnesses and my kindnesses in this sedulous contempt. My inversions decorate an underlying irreversibility, or at least that's the dream. I'm working with hideous sources, but I'm better than that; I'm going to make everything do exactly what I want and it's going to be beguiling and transformative, as divinely prepossessing as your pious consort squatting to take a piss in the rain, as comely as anyone young and perfect and pierced in the right places. This is going to be a barbarian summer.

I spent the first years of my life as your average aristocrat. I wasn't planning on going into hiding. Nobody we knew did that. Nobody even talked about people who weren't like us. My parents, my parent's friends, they caught on to the proximity of the less affluent and the irreligious like you would a gas leak. Rule was: we can feel your pain just fine through our rubber gloves.

I get so distracted from my own life, it's like the world goes on without me. Only one of many conspiracies I have to resist: they need me out in the open and they'll do anything. But they don't seem to get it, way too lost in the hunt: make me exoteric and it'll all be over, find me and I'm gone. And so what if the chances of being driven mad by 5G are directly correlated to your being half-mad already. And how can I be expected to think when even the air's infected with mistrust? I need the blinds pulled down and a commonplace silence made of background noise not so different from no noise at all. I need to be wooed back from the long, dark corridor I've entered. Do I have to die as well before somebody listens, before somebody somewhere sees I'm missing for a reason?

The nobility don't get to retire. How beautiful it must be to die in secret – and live that way too. My bad back is penance for the splendour of all those parties. I'll take the accoutrements of privilege to the moon, to the bombed-out storefronts in Tehran, to those smouldering Syrian ruins where my only camouflage will be the extent of the population already underground. I'm outstretched like a sacrificial symbol. I have homemade amulets against getting caught. If they find out where I am, I'll be someone else before anyone can tell.

I'm looking at the enormous ears of some elderly man. The flesh is yellowish and glossy. I deliberately forget the French term, the idiom for a shell. I was a churchgoer, I whisper. I did everything right. You wouldn't believe how predisposed to luxury I was. I had nearly a lifetime of making plans for the man I became. I was flapping around like an injured bird and not one of them noticed. A fire might have broken out at any time. It took nearly a lifetime to destroy myself in the process.

Thing is, you don't get to reinvent yourself when other people contain bits of who you are. You can't disappear and leave others behind still wearing your face. I stood at the top of the stairs knowing I would never see them again.

And yet somehow it seemed we were more intimately connected than before. I say a separate prayer for each one of them – and while I mention the dogs, I stop short of individual devotions. Speciesist, I know, but the dogs are not part of the equation: their ages do not count.

Their expressions were oblivious to the bullet holes. For a while I made them my confidantes. When it was over, the cuticles on both hands were discoloured. I'd reached the age of 50 without ever having scrubbed them with bleach, with Swarfega, with any harsh abrasives, and that it should all come undone. It's a dangerous thing to get exposed to your appetites. How many more have to die before we rehabilitate our craving for the nebulous? Do you think I wanted it this way? To have to do that to be the person I was already? Why did nobody recognize me as this unsolved problem before it came to this? And with only traces left now of being any selfsame man.

I wished no harm to my family. For years I went on as if I could survive the otherworldliness of my transparency like everyone else. I couldn't know that, because I'd shot animals before, my finger would remember the trigger so well. I don't hate God and God doesn't hate me. We're close that way. Come the evening I still nod off in my chair. I was bequeathed the resting heartrate of a 13-year-old boy, and I plan to use it wisely.

Their combined age was 115. Divided by 5 that's 23. The number 23 is so weird it has its own enigma. And while you can come up with coincidences for virtually any number, 23 takes the crown. The list of advocates for its oddness are diverse and impressive: William Burroughs, Anton Wilson, Albert Einstein, Jim Carey. I had

less than two months before the numbers went wrong:
Benoît would be 14 and that would be that.

I find a video of my garden on the website of an English newspaper. It is only 24 seconds long. (I took this
extra second for a tease. I freeze on the 23rd second and
the male gendarme is smiling.) I watch it repeatedly for
an hour or more with no thought for how eccentric this
might look, and how while my IP is hidden the encryp-
tion is not as secure as it could be.

COUNT TERROR

I THINK I'M IN THE WRONG PLACE.

I heard someone say how when I kill people I get to feed on their afterlives. Apparently, I insert my right index finger into the holes in their heads, and this is supposed to connect me to their deceased states. Ha! Ridiculous! Not it at all. I remember thinking how quaint this sounded compared with what really happened, and how laughably unlike my true motivations. I mean, I have indeed been experientially connected to my biological children in physiologically abnormal ways, that much is true. Their mental lives had played out inside my head alongside my own since before they were born. To describe, if I can: it was less like split screen video and more like tendrils. And I think you'll say I overestimated my ability to fracture my awareness and still maintain the integrity of a single life, that I needn't have had three children before deciding I couldn't take it. And it's true I could have allowed my wife and adoptive son to live and achieved the same psychological ends, but that would have been cruel, to leave them that way, and I am not a cruel person.

I ask you, do I look the type to murder my family for no good reason?

I'd tried other ways to get them out. A kind of scraping technique, like taking mud off the bottom of a shoe, but with intrusive thoughts, whole streams of them – tendrils of disgusting, artificial nonsense folding over and into each other like a French plait.

I know how many strange deaths it takes to do things properly.

Their lives were so dull, so godless and uninspired. How could I possibly have had children with such sickly minds? Someone was playing a revolting game. Why couldn't they have been more interesting? Oh what's the use?

I wonder, do I come here often?

In honour of my poet ancestor Alphonse de Lamartine, I wrote a one line sonnet with seven voltas. When I tried to find it afterwards I couldn't. The words had gone and erased themselves, and I was done then with all this talk of going mad. I wasn't that way. Even the mad poets weren't mad. We were twitchier than the others perhaps, kept reality dangling on a longer string, but the clinical diagnosis was nothing more than libellous expediency. We weren't the poisoned rivers covered with hair they wanted us to be. Our minds were not pigs caught in spider webs screaming because their muscles were on fire. If we were all funambulists all of the time, then we were the only ones who knew it.

The handsome boy was made to look exactly like Benoît for reasons directly connected to the pearl-handled penknife I minutes later slid into the side of his neck. His posing for all the world as the above-ground variant of my exquisitely formed but irrefutably subterranean son was just the kind of offensive injunction

I couldn't ignore. Something impelled me to push what was already indistinguishable to this very edge.

I imagine fathers worldwide just upping and killing their families. After that they leave. They all go to the same place, but I can't work out where that is, our familial indiscretions only establishing the most rudimentary behavioural network.

Not only do I lack resistance to the present, but I resist the lack of all temporal modes. At the same time, I undermine my entire enterprise with a poorly chosen idiom.

The way it goes, if I imagine all my finest moments to be opiate-induced, no imagination is ever required. There's such unhappiness in unsubstantiated illusion that we're forced to swim sometimes in reservoirs of our own blood.

I often wonder if SIDS wouldn't have been kinder. For everyone. But what is kindness but a way of saying life is a mistake? I resist all peritectic points. I resist easy answers, especially the ones that are difficult.

Alone in The Bunker I get to make all the strange noises I like. Erato shits and I moil inside it like a silly worm. A man-worm silly with the spasm in his toes, clawing and spreading like a forest skink's, squealing for the walls to hear, refined like mitochondrial Eve was not my mother. My mother was a maenad mistakenly born Catholic. When I was a boy, her chides were intoxicated with a false notion of purity. She wore real fur like she'd skinned the animals herself.

There's a positive correlation between dreaming of breathlessness and dying in hibernation.

How is it Melpomene farts and I get bad breath?

We met at Tanztheater. I said you looked like a starved and stumbling dog crammed into the body of a bird. You seemed pleased. I pretended to be human till I bled.

I'm in a boat in the middle of the ocean feeling increasingly pyromaniacal.

Although the fingerprints were somehow mine, my DNA was not found inside a man detained at Glasgow airport having just flown in from Roissy-Charles-de-Gaulle. He had never lived in Nantes, had not been missing for eight years, since 2011, was not the inscrutable *monstre* of any French city. He'd not once withdrawn cash from an ATM in Roquebrune-sur-Argens in Var. He had an alibi for the 14th and 15th of April, and did not own a bag that could conceal a rifle like mine. In Limay, French authorities find a different man: a septuagenarian with a Scottish wife and his own passport. The false denunciation remains anonymous and unexplained, like me.

Ordinary middle-class family still stings. What had I done to them to deserve that? They knew my lineage. My royal blood sold their papers. I was a bigger story than that English prince and his underage girls. Even now there's this accusation of ordinariness. What do I have to do? How many times must I escape?

Although, I do so adore a manhunt. It remains one of the few ways left to be alive. And because I've long been a student of all the well-documented cases, the fictionalized ones as well as the real, a certain amount of bleed, being inevitable, can be evidenced throughout. I suppose I've been working on the mores of my cadre of absconders since I was a child, started aestheticizing fugitive tendencies since before I knew what I was doing had anything to do with organizing the biographic mess of these intriguingly liminal types.

I can't remember at this stage whether or not it was me who sent that picture of my boys to Agence France-Presse. The writing on the back – "I am still alive. From then until this hour" – looks like mine alright, but I can't say for sure. The sign off seems authentic too. And it might have been me. A crudely scrawled thing such as it is, mostly in capitals, becomes an innominate means of exposure, identifying its cause as a language-user with an inclusivity so predeterminably vague as to be almost useless as a tool to distinguish me from any other baseline human intelligence.

Gerhard flies out from he forgets where to Incheon International in Seoul on a fake passport. The idea is to visit all the locations in the film *Burning*. He stands outside the building containing Shin Hae-mi's apartment and masturbates. He goes to Paju, near the North Korean border. He kills ten boys and sets them on fire. Nobody notices. The smoke drifts for miles.

I was last seen leaving the hotel Formule 1 in Roquebrune-sur-Argens on foot with a rifle on my back. Some of them can't wait to mention how it's a budget hotel, reduce my status even further: just look at what the aristocracy's become. I told them I was a secret agent; I told them I was entering witness protection. What's so odd about a secret agent with a weapon? I have a licence for whatever it is a gun is for. What's so odd about a DEA informant turned protected witness you can't find?

I like hearing how we appeared happy. The perfected family and now look. I like hearing how it is I appear to other people, how they can feel so confident about making snap summations about the neurochemical secretions in my head. We were so ordinary and happy and seemingly middle class in the House of Terror. So aristocratic and well-respected and murdered and murderous. Like royalty isn't bloodthirsty by definition.

Why is it always their decomposing remains that are found, when I'm their decomposing remains, and I'm still at large? I escape inside their pickled skins, their limpid structures softened till all you'll see is me: I compose their collective decomposition into a purgatorial swelling, an irascible pronunciamento of privilege and despondent idiocy.

I'm the main suspect, but I might not have done it. This could be some *Three Days of the Condor* type thing: I come home to find my family slaughtered, I grab my rifle for protection and I flee.

You shoot a howling Labrador to stop the howling. What's so hard to understand about that? Whether I shot them or not, I couldn't have taken them with me. Can't do walkies where I'm at.

Drugged to induce sleep and then a couple of bullets to the head: this is the work of someone who cares. Perhaps a coward too. You need to ask whether I am either one of these things?

I inherited the .22 rifle from my father when he died. It's the same calibre as the gun used to kill my family. The shame of the dwindled family estate and my own dire financial worries is thought to be all the catalyst a fragile ego like mine – an aristocrat like me, descended from French royalty (wait, did I mention that already?) – needed to embark on this most heinous spree killing. Why else would I buy a silencer for the gun? Don't I have sensitive ears, in keeping with the rest of me? If cadaver dogs ever find out where I am, I'll hear them coming. And don't forget, as a good citizen, I always consider my neighbours.

They give the order of the murders as Arthur, Anne, Benoît, Agnès, and then Thomas later. It's supposedly incriminating that Thomas and I went out for dinner and barely spoke. If we'd been English nobody would have noticed. The fact that food is so closely associated with socializing in French culture is being held against me. The xenophobia of the media is beyond. Also, consider the order at La Croix Cadeau in Avrillé: a €35 tasting menu with half a bottle of Anjou-villages-brissac red wine for me, and for Thomas the sea bass and a tomato juice, coming to a total of a mere €72.55. For a last meal I would have insisted he have the steak (a Polmard 2000 vintage cote de boeuf, no less), the wine would have been a good year, the best year they had. I'm French nobility for fuck's sake. Will no one give me some credit here? I may be a spree killer, but do I have to be cheap as well?

I drove south afterwards. I like to drive south. France is a beautiful country, and spring in the south has such a mollifying sway on my temper. Nothing can be done to me there.

The police searched the caves and abandoned lead and potassium mines around Roquebrune-sur-Argens. There's deep woodland in that area and they trawled it for weeks looking for my suicided body. By the time they got there I'd gone. I wasn't there. I might have exited by train or by boat or ship. I was not found. I will never be found.

I've read what Agnès supposedly wrote in some on-line chatroom: how unhappy she was, what a draconian bully I am, how cold and authoritarian, how little money we had. It could be true. She could be surly now and then. I don't know: didn't everyone say how happy we were? Everyone can't be wrong. That almost never happens.

I'm supposed to be sequestered in one of my extended family's many luxurious properties. And yet someone saw me in Italy, Chicago, Moldova…

I miss my mistress in Paris. She was good to me when everyone else was getting on with their lives. She let me shit in her mouth instead of saying goodbye. I used to do a lot of squats and running. I bet your pussy grip, she said as a joke – spotlighting the comparative lowliness of her birth as a kind of funny. I went along; I broke her pinky finger in more places than I thought possible.

They think I sold my wife's jewellery to fund my escape. That never happened. Sometimes I play dress-up. I wear the trinkets of hers that fit. I cram the rings onto the first phalanx of whatever finger. I've fed the pearls up my arse on numerous occasions (saltwater naturals, I could feel the quality), fastened white gold bracelets round my genitals till I could see all the variously coloured veins.

Buying quicklime is incriminating. Like the speed and smell of someone's decomposition is an issue for me. I can see how it looks. It looks bad for sure. And then there's the cement, the bullets, the cleaning supplies, garbage bags, spade, and trolley. I look like the bad man who offed his family in a burst of premeditated vanity. Can I help the way I looked back then? You should see me now, though. The plastic surgeon's done wonders with my nascent jowls. I'm so full of Botox I never have to smile again.

The trail, they say, went cold. The morons expected to apprehend me within the week, but that's because they're morons. "I think I've got a superiority complex, you could call it that. I belong to a group of people who are intelligent, determined, balanced and in good moral and physical health. Such people are rare compared to the masses." This is something I'd say. And if I wasn't so clever and so proficient at concealment my rarity would let me down. My exceptional nature would be my undoing. The arrogance of Leopold and Loeb should be a lesson to us all. And by "all" I mean of course virtually no one.

I could have pretended to be Thomas if I'd wanted. I can write like an inferior version of myself without trying. My superiority is plastic. I can be anyone I choose. Just yesterday I drank Coke from the can. If they noticed it wasn't him, it was because they were supposed to notice. And if they were supposed to notice, what is it that they're missing?

And what about those good, honest Nantes types who had spoken to my wife even after she'd been drugged and shot twice in the head? I wonder what they talked about. I think they were probably polite enough not to mention the bullet holes, the quicklime, or the fact that the dog she was walking was dead.

I am sometimes my sister and her husband on Reddit. They are sometimes themselves. We take it in turns. Between us I am always innocent, always truthful, always France's own and ever-loyal Xavier.

In 2018, French police raided a monastery thinking I was someone who turned out to be just another monk. Apparently he looked enough like me to warrant their efforts. Maybe they mistook the rosary teasing his colon for my wife's pearls. Maybe they mistook his vow of silence for guilt.

I was born into the opulent vomit of Versailles. You could say I was made for it. Rigid, upper-class, Catholic, stuffy, conformist: everything a burgeoning spree killer needs to make a start.

When I was about ten my father left Versailles. For whatever reason he didn't take me with him. I lived with my grandmother. She lunched at expensive restaurants and drunk cognac from a cut glass schooner. I never once heard her fart, but sometimes I would smell her. The hair she wore was kept together with various types of gold pin. I was lonely and would sometimes imagine having sex with her.

I was twenty when I first met Agnès. She made an impression: it was like looking in a mirror and knowing the reflection would fuck you back. I didn't want to get married right away, I wanted to go somewhere first, do something else. When I got back she had Arthur inside her, but I married her anyway. I took him on as if he were my own son. I was bigger than Versailles. I was progressive. I was selflessly modern.

If we'd have been allowed to move to Florida things might have been different. Although different might have been worse. Who knows? My family might have killed me, fed me to the dogs. I might have fed entire busloads of schoolchildren to the gators over a number of years and never been caught. You just can't tell. Anyway, we settled in Nantes instead of any of that.

Whenever I hear music I think of Thomas. He was studying music when I was still pretending not to know what that was. I was making jokes of it, the ephemeral unworldliness of such a boy. He didn't even fight back when I punched him, an embarrassment, a son of mine. And Agnès reporting me to the police. Her baby with a few cuts and bruises, his precious ears for his precious music a little swollen for a few days. And Anne modelling for those mail-order catalogues with her grades, doing it to spite me for the money we didn't have, threatening to parade her skin next but without actually saying it. The looks she'd give me giving her away. La Perverie turns out slut after slut, a conveyor belt of girls dreaming of fucking God and then settling for the first dick that comes their way. Devoutly wet between the legs like her mother.

I read I'm "too judgmental, too quick to argue, too rigid, too military, [how] there's no more tenderness between us [Agnès and me], no more attention, no softness, no sex..." She wants me to put out in return for her family's money, is that it? Like I'm a fucking whore. Like I can get hard on demand for any kind of body, a body loosened into a sloppy kind of nothing by four babies and nearly five decades. Softness? It was her softness I couldn't stomach.

Agnès says she asked me if I was happy and I replied: "Yes I am, but if we could all die tomorrow, that would be better." It's not true. I said yesterday. I would have said yesterday. Tomorrow is always too late.

To the allegations of heartlessness I give you €50,000, borrowed from my Parisian paramour to give to Agnès, to give to our children, to continue the life we had for a little longer. Didn't I say "I am awake almost every night with these morbid ideas. Burning down the house after giving everyone sleeping pills, or killing myself so that Agnès gets €600,000," or some such amount? And isn't that a kind of love? Every day felt "radical and final," and yet still I simulated the future we were going to have. Wasn't the resolve I found to keep us afloat a declaration of sorts, a difficult, intricate poem of intent? I could have cut your throats and left you out for the birds.

All bills paid in full before our made-up move to Australia. Those private schools got the last of their blood money. I sent in my wife's resignation, excused her gastroenteritis. My new job in the Antipodes remains a mystery. My employment opportunities there could have been any number of things.

On April 3rd we were all seen having a happy dinner. Except Arthur, Arthur wasn't there. But the rest of us were in a restaurant together laughing and smiling. It's a shame the kids (the babies, Anne and Benoît) were ill the next day, but it happens. I don't think it was the food. They haven't been seen alive since, but I don't think the food had anything to do with it.

The police visited our house six times over a period of three weeks before they discovered the bodies. Five times they came and went, finding nothing of any real concern, and then all of a sudden these dead people turn up. And they'd read/written that letter, so they knew where to put them. A few pictures were missing, the beds were stripped, but no blood, no signs of violence. And yet my wife's family kept insisting something was wrong. Sounds like something they'd do.

55 Boulevard Robert-Schuman, Nantes rebranded as a House of Terror. Two graves under the terrace under a concrete screed, a patio: one containing Thomas and the other containing the rest. I supposedly wrapped them in blankets and placed religious icons next to their bodies. They imagine I performed some kind of ceremony – with my cock out and elastic bands cinching my balls said someone on Reddit. It never happened, any of it.

I'd drugged all the children before shooting them twice in the back of the head. Agnès was shot the same way but not drugged. Had I wanted her to be aware of what I was doing? Or if she was asleep, and I did her first, then I suppose she wouldn't need to be drugged. But they didn't find any blood spatter on her sleep apnea machine, so establishing the exact order of the killings is still a game you can play.

I had a three week head start on the police. You can go a long way in three weeks. The conjecture is I planned to kill myself. Why else would I not try to conceal my escape, allow myself to be caught on CCTV, a speed camera, check into hotels, etc.? Why else but to lead you to an array of abandoned mines and dense woodland, to the Massif des Maures, where you'd spend weeks looking for my dead body, thinking I'd be there in the undergrowth like Jacques Massié and his family, found murdered in 1981.

I stayed in the house for a week after the murders. I lived in the house – ran errands, posted stuff online, sent emails, defecated, pissed, ate, drunk, whatever else – with my dead family buried in the back garden.

There has been a very big mistake in Scotland. Ha. Police are dumb the world over, but the Scots are going for the top spot. Mr Joao looks nothing like me, he's Portuguese, he has a finger missing. They thought all this was part of some elaborate disguise.

Why would I travel 200 miles to buy bin liners and plastic paving slabs? Why would I make a seven hour round trip to a DIY store in Saint-Maur to cover my tracks, and then leave the receipt in my house for the police to find? Why would I then buy four 10 kg bags of lime from local stores?

I had a business, based in Pornic, called SELREF, whose purpose has been called "secretive and ambiguously defined." Much is made of the six sales staff I hired and let go soon after. Some ventures, apparently, require a level of trust that is not easily fulfilled.

I'm clearly attracted to Parisian women: in addition to the salacious speculation about the living arrangements of my lover, my wife was born in the suburbs of Paris, in Neuilly-sur-Seine. What part of that girl was left in the woman teaching the Catechism to minors at Blanche-de-Castille Catholic School in Nantes remains unclear.

I have a precise definition of catastrophe that does not include a family succumbing to its own inevitable logic, however barbaric and evil-seeming that sounds.

Fabrice, my inquisitive neighbour, says he saw me putting several large bags into my car around the time of the murders. As someone who invests far too much energy in the goings-on of others, his testimony must be taken seriously.

I talked to my sister, Christine, on the phone for half an hour and she said I seemed normal. "I'm putting the kids to bed" needn't have any murky connotations.

The bailiff turns up on April 5th for his 20 grand. I didn't need to have slaughtered my family not to answer the door.

The messages I supposedly sent out to the family might, as my lawyer Stéphane Goldenstein points out, been written under duress. Either I killed myself or I was murdered (and disposed of elsewhere to incriminate me forever).

I did get Thomas to leave his friend's house and come home. His mother had come off her bike and was in some not insignificant discomfort. We thought he'd want to know. A good boy: he wanted to come home as soon as he heard.

The women who say they saw my wife after she'd been shot in the head are telling the truth. They correlated the chance encounters with concrete events and dates from their own routines. They do not believe they can be wrong and neither do I. But if it wasn't my wife under the patio, who was it? I suppose there are lots of dead women, so you could just use one of them. Or make your own. Dead women are such easy currency.

They found my metallic blue Citroën C5 in the car park of the Formule 1 hotel. What kind of aristocrat drives a car like that? Or stays in a hotel like that? Or puts holes in the heads of his family because he's financially

embarrassed like that? I should mention though how
I spent the night of April 12th in a better hotel, in the
Auberge de Cassagne in Le Pontet in Vaucluse. I used a
false name, but it was definitely me (you can check): I am
Mr Laurent Xavier. It cost a more respectable €214.59.

I called my old girlfriend (let's not say her name) on
the 13th when I was in La Seyne-sur-Mer in Var. I lived
there for a while in the 80s with no thought of murder-
ing anyone much. She says I made contact but that she
never met me. I understand why she'd say that. What
right-minded woman wants to admit to fucking a man
who had only days before massacred his family for no
good reason anyone could think of?

Our relatives were advised not to view the bodies.
They complied and now no one knows who they buried.
The bodies were disinterred, cremated and then buried
again quickly before they changed their minds, before they
thought to check that the dead people were their dead people. Now they'll never know. My side of the family is very
suspicious. They now doubt the truth of the official story.
They don't believe Agnès and the kids were killed at all.
Cremation is a good way to cover your tracks.

I read that around 1,400 people attended their fu-
neral. There were no flowers or wreaths. I think everyone followed the protocols associated with such events.
Most faces looked serious or emotional, respectfully
fluctuating between the two. Some even cried. The
voices were quieter and softer than they would have
been in everyday life. This is to be expected. The tone
throughout was respectfully sober. Some sat there fud-
dled by the realisation that not everyone lives forever.

There was the usual bored child that had to be bribed or chastised into being quiet and/or sitting still. This child had not yet learnt how to take death seriously, how to pretend you aren't bored or amused by the risible spectacle of cultured grief.

Members of the public, hundreds of them, godless cattle that they are, took it upon themselves to document my internet history: every Facebook post and comment, the forums I contributed to, etc. They did the same for Agnès. They put all the words together and worked out who we were.

Apparently, the police spent two years looking for an ex of mine called Claudia because we were once nearly married. She's described as a German woman. They say we kept in contact all these years. Judge Robert Tchalian was fixated on her relevance. I don't think they ever found her.

I had many identities on La Cité catholique. No one on that forum liked answering my questions, and they would block me, so I'd come back as someone else. Imagine all those fundamentalist Catholics and not one of them understood the first thing about sacrifice. Bernard Blandre claims my motives, whatever they were, were not religious. But he's an idiot: everything is religious. The shit I took this morning reproduced the very face of the Virgin Mary. Yesterday it was Christ himself. Men like me do not need to go to church. Church is for women and queers. I'm so full of God you could eat me like a banana.

My company Netsurf Concept LLC in Florida was founded in 1998. We facilitated anonymity. You think you disappear this well on a whim?

In June 2013 they found the body of a man in Draguignan that, because it was so close to where I was last seen, they thought might be me. The autopsy they performed was inconclusive, so they could not completely rule out the possibility that the body was indeed the very same Xavier Dupont de Ligonnès. As it stands, that dead body might still turn out to be me. Another body was discovered in a forest in Bagnols-en-Forêt, near Fréjus, but when they found a metal pin in the deceased man's forearm, and someone else's DNA on objects in the encampment, they discontinued this line of enquiry. It's an odd feeling when you might be some dead person you've never met.

My sister Christine and her husband Bertram have not wavered in their protestations of my innocence. She sticks to the version of events where we all left for America because our lives were under threat in France, and that the bodies found at our house cannot be those of Agnès and the children. She claims that "the information leaked to the media originates from sources with an interest in making the family disappear." They have fulfilled "my hope that, even after a police investigation, my parents, brothers and sisters will never be led to believe that I intentionally caused these accidents (even if the evidence is strong)."

The family lawyer, Mr Goldenstein, has remained loyal beyond all letter of the law. He fixed his attention on the pertinent facts and refused to even glance in the direction of the more widely accepted speculations fast becoming consensus amongst the media and its consumers. Deeply concerned about how we have only the

vaguest idea of when they were killed, the autopsy establishing a window of ten to twenty-one days between
burial and exhumation, he goes on to venture that all we
really know is that there were bodies found at my house
and that those bodies share the same DNA, without
stipulating whether or not said DNA was shared with
me or Agnès. There is also the discrepancy of the bodies' heights and weights, which do not match the known
dimensions and mass of my wife and children, and the
implausibility of one man on his hands and knees digging a hole of that size, a displacement of earth totalling
some 2.5 cubic metres. (I mean, just how was I supposed
to have buried their bodies in such a space, with less
than 4ft from the ground to work in, meaning I would
have had to excavate all that soil on my hands and knees
without proper tools, and without leaving any displaced
earth behind? Christine tells them about my bad back,
about the recurring pains in my neck. She highlights
how someone digging in the cramped space would have
certainly banged their head at some point, and yet no
skin cells or blood or DNA was ever discovered on the
underside of the terrace.)

Goldenstein concludes: "I don't know who killed this
family. Nothing about their lives would lead me to believe that anyone would have it in for them to this extent.
That is the conclusion of my clients. Since no one could
have killed them, the fact is that they are not dead." The
logic here is incontrovertible, and surprisingly good for a
member of the legal profession.

I have been sighted on over 900 separate occasions all
over the world. I can't say how many of these are true.

LITTLE SUICIDE
PICTURE

I MISS MY DADDY. DAVID BERKOWITZ SAID THAT. I was living in London and mostly unhappy. I had come to expect exactly nothing of interest. Almost no one had ever heard of me. I had money but you couldn't sell me the want. I had a girlfriend you could sell anything, who said things like I'm not intimidated by caterpillars apropos of just about anything, and who ate the scale from my kettle like she'd invented the Eucharist. If I committed a crime at that point, it was more through tiredness than need.

The sky every day was painful. I sat at my window looking out. I was on storey 31 and the city was beneath me, along with everything else. I spoke in mouthfuls, words I'd collected until no more would fit: conscientious vixens choking on their cubs, mummy birds clogged up with worms. I didn't miss my daddy. I didn't miss anyone, but I was looking for a person I'd imagined – a person I could miss. My girlfriend at some point was wrapping her head in tinfoil because she thought it was funny. I think she mistook my sighs for a kind of laughter, but I explained how I'm not idiosyncratic that way – never have been. I aspire to be more transparent, you see, more rigorously see-through. I was looking for someone I would find. It can happen like that.

It's January and I smoke cigarettes like it's 1950 and the world still loves a smoker. I smoke like Dennis Potter dying in an interview with Melvyn Bragg, drinking morphine and smoking like it means more than it does. I've committed some indiscretion, the severity of which I'm keeping vague. So what of small rooms, of afternoons, the drizzle outside bending the world? So what of bare electric lights and my pervert's eyes? I have fatal heart attacks by the dozen. I have an itching to lapse into something more than this compulsory unease.

One time, I introspected so hard I went through and out the other side. I ended up where I was. I ended up second-hand again. I was thinking too loudly at this point. I had all the signs of a false haunting. My girl-friend was copying a detail from a painting by R. B. Kitaj onto her thigh in felt tip. It was *Little Suicide Picture* from 1968 and she drew the prostrate figure with the S on its head. Then she drew an S on her own head like that was enough, like I'd know what to do next. I say, Don't ask a friend to suicide for you – it's impolite. And we look at each other like we're both protagonists, unlearning our lines before it's too late. That you got there quicker came down to how much more the food you ate tasted exactly like food.

I was having trouble sitting at a window just looking out. Clouds, sky, blankness: I was crumbling. There was joy with undertones of what was also intolerable, and I recognized it because I always define art this way. It's dreary, I know, talking about sensations like they add up, but I'm sucking air through smaller and smaller apertures same as the rest of you.

And my VR Headset is switched off. I'm seeing in the dark. Just the apparatus, nothing else. Everything I touch is part of this deformed thing I'm becoming. It's dreary, I know, but blurred was the aesthetic back then. Don't vilify me for being no more tragically inclined than your average shrieking toddler. My inadequacies are too many, but imagining the universe cares enough to make my acquaintance isn't one of them. As inadequacies go, mine are reversible – like a cheap raincoat: watch me wear my emotional frailty as the ultimate super-power. Mad thing is, I only spiral into yet more sanity.

Actually, since I've mentioned it already, I'm something of a connoisseur of shrieks. And I can tell the ones that emanate from a place that no amount of good fortune will ever cleanse. When I hear one of those I'm instantly in love. I have to check myself, or else I have the shrieker in an embrace from which it's sometimes difficult for their lungs to recover in time. And that it comes from a good place can be a hard sell when all you want is air, and it's everywhere and refusing to come true.

At a gallery showcasing the work of new artists I'd never heard of, I liked how all of them were trying so hard to be by-products of some intimacy they were yet to experience. I felt lunged at and overly speculative for the time of day. The lights in there were kind of writhing, and I got to thinking how small my girlfriend had become in light of how she was dead. It was sad. I experienced new areas of sensitivity during this time. I replaced all my former cynicisms with a kind of patriotism for her lost body. All I did was regurgitate this gloomy plant, these rootless leaves, turning slowly brown since she'd stopped wanting to grow. And there I was an émigré from her crazed expectations of being alive. I thought I might honour her with whatever I decided to do next. I thought I might love something for once. For all my delight in whatever provocations, I would bring myself to heel.

I want to go somewhere where there are waves. I want to time how broken I am by the sound of them breaking. That sounded like love when I thought it up. If she came back now would she stare at me the same way, the way kids do it, the impertinence of not caring how intrusive their eyes can be? If words aren't meant to have meaning, the S on her forehead was only one small part of a wider distraction.

I met her in a room in which she wasn't expecting to meet anyone. We both laughed. I think we both laughed. I laughed, then she laughed. I don't think she wanted to laugh, though. Oh well.

ELEPHANT
DECOMPOSED

WHERE DO I START WHEN IT MAKES SO LITTLE difference?

I was trying on costumes when I went soft. I was all kinds of pretty girls before that. Dancing usually keeps me warm; only, when I stop I can always feel the sweat. The windows in my room preplastic and rattling, so that when the cold gets in I feel it on the skin parts. It pimples round the scars, and the scars stay flat. I only have a few, but where they intersect I like the patterns they make. The cold air though makes me sore. Usually, at that time, I'm in jungles and far-off places with my predawn eyes. My vision clearing to a picture on my wall of two pregnant bellies with the babies showing through.

There was nothing for thousands of miles, just me coming ashore in the slinkiest dress I could find. I'm draped in the finest explosives with nowhere left to blow up. I come in on the ferry. The city's an elephant all rotted out, set on fire, groaning and pissed like it never had a woman. When the monsoon starts I'll regain my sense of wonder, always happens that way. I always get too excited and forget, but I have moments of joy like the rest of you, like the finest and the stupidest of creatures. My problem is I'm everywhere at once.

Come rainy season I'm taking ten hits a day. I'm not sure how long a day is, it all depends. I have a love interest over on the south side, but all he does now is eat, and the way he looks at me isn't healthy. All time eat, says his mother, a kitchen lackey when she bothers, a potato peeler, and never seen *King Kong* or *Sunset Boulevard* or pre-colour Hollywood anywhere but the posters in her tiny back room. Wiry body like a boy's and hair you could hide a kitten in. More than forty years, grunting, ghostly, a clot of foggy weather drifting through rooms, and still nothing to confess. So sunk, so aimless: I love her as if she were my own mother. I go to kiss her sometimes and she laughs like she doesn't secretly want me to fuck her.

I'm not vindictive: I only kill anyone. People like me. It's my terrorist tendency, after all, to make up for all this wasted time: I've overslept, missed half my life.

We like each other's fashionable nonsense: his Prada frames and lip gloss priced by the limb, my underwear stolen from the wash lines of the richest neighbourhoods.

I was getting lazy. I looked for ways to discipline myself. But then it smacked too much of the pleasure I was avoiding, so I stopped. When he's flat back on the bed with his arms folded behind his head his unwashed pits look like house spiders rolled into balls. I'm crazy for the smell of them. He has quotes from French- and German-language poets all over his ribs and across his stomach. I lick the words and put my fingers inside him. Hölderlin always makes my tongue go numb. I feel him again when I swallow. It tingles. I live in a room above a nail bar owned by two Korean women. When I sleep in I can hear them shellacking my dreams.

I'm perfused with disbelief. I should really be confined to a clinic for ongoing treatment, where someone with an American-born wife and a manageable sense of hopelessness can take my confession for the next 30 years and pronounce me cured on my deathbed.

If I get the death penalty it'll be too late. I'm grandiloquently unrealistic, but it's the only reality I know. Because of this I come across as overexposed. I've heard them say it, how I'm hard to look at sometimes. Because of this I've survived as nobody in particular, and everybody else. I can't compute how many without mutilating the figures.

I'd like to be indifferent to aging, but when you look as good as I look… He was a great-looking kid when I put the gun into the small of his back and … I kissed him on the mouth afterwards. He tasted of the mints he'd been eating. I'm tired of reading about the untimeliness of death. Death is never early, never late. It always knows just when to arrive.

We are approaching empty. My days are there already. I spent them spread across the floor. It was too warm at night for loneliness and more brutal fantasies and refashioning my shame. When the music started up again I was like concrete. I was trying to score some Larkin on his neck. On reflection, the bubbling was a clue. I was a chronicler of anguish when no one cared about anguish anymore. In mirrors, I reflected badly on how little he was moving, but he looked good, shiny and smooth as a mango.

I'm a runaway without a home. Imagine having a homeland. Imagine the confidence; imagine the stupidity.

I hoped the autobiographical glut would amount to something, the ultimate act of the anonymous everyone – a ghost still haunted by its body. I'd be dispassionately passionate, passionately dispassionate, joyous in my despair and despairing in my joy. In distorting clarity I'd be lucid to a fault; I'd articulate distortion while at my most deranged. I'd impose order haphazardly, reduce chaos to a grid. Unrestrained by the logic of time and place, I'd leave the entire fabric of whatever this is part-chewed, barely hanging together, bedraggled like a paper effigy left out in the rain.

All this connectivity is making me lonely; everyone's loneliness is what we have in common, all connected in our failure to connect. It's why I want to solve the world. Why I want you to love me

PRIMATERNITY

I hear things like this and all the joy is gone. I don't even want to breathe anymore, not if it's to hear more things like this. Feels like a state-controlled programme conceived to make me cut my throat already. And if I was more paranoid, less resilient, not pre-soaked in despair since before I could remember, then maybe my habits would be different. Maybe I wouldn't be glancing into mirrors expecting to see someone else. Maybe I wouldn't be quite so immune to the misdirection of my self-loathing. Maybe the days wouldn't be this horrible liquid, crawling uphill with no sense of where it came from.

I'm buried next to myself. It's the way I compare a rule to what instantiates it. I've been reborn so many times I'm my only surviving blood relative – and it's not as if I even know if it's possible to exist anymore. I had thoughts yesterday no mother could absolve. They rolled around in my head all day like prisoners on the floor of the Bridgewater State Hospital. I have headaches that expand into the world and make the people around me ill. They don't know it yet, but my neighbours are all slowly dying of me. I used to have pets until the brain cancers got them one by one. I'd say I find it hard to live if I knew what that meant.

It was a catalogue and there were pictures: pygmy marmosets, tarsier, titi, squirrel, saki and capuchin monkeys. I'd read the shopping list of favoured species before thinking to look away. And there were pictures of their short-haired, fetal bodies, and those o-so-darling oversized nocturnal eyes. I wondered: where they were going, was there anything they could see? Was it possible for light to reach inside as far as that? And then, squeamish either way, found I had no impetus to know.

How they were adapted to fit made me want to weep. The tails, which can be twice as long or more as the rest of the monkey, were the first to be removed. And then every tooth and then every nail. And then the anaesthetic wore off, and no eyes were built for what it left. My fellow-feeling for these tiny beings touched me like I was any kind of human who felt things for other things as if I were them – an extension of my self-interest, if you will. And this apparition of me nontransparent for once, and so much less the vacuole I'd come to unknow. I saw it moving and caring and following me about, dark and vaporous and leech-like, a more tangible version of whatever I was whenever I thought that way.

Post-natal depression attracted the wrong kind of friends. It happens. They sat round in circles drinking coffee and tea and cannibalizing each other's traumas. Their gossip was a feverish collaboration, each one pretending to be further from recovery than the one before. The terrible thing about the violation of their being-without-child was how habitual it had become. Some of them pretended to be more insignificant than they were, which was the most difficult thing they'd ever done – and the most significant.

They regarded sex without babies as a violent simulation. They compared it to bulimia: the more they had the emptier they became. With the help of inertia and deep-fried food, most became too ugly even to masturbate. They exposed themselves in too many chatrooms at once, came away with the feeling that no one cared, not like they did on TV, where people got paid to behave like the real thing.

In case you didn't know, for some women the being pregnant part is precisely where it's at: the material promise of it, the feel of a life moving inside them, all of it unsurpassable. There's nothing comes close to growing your own painkillers. And don't creators always make the best destroyers?

The most pregnant of the bunch smoked a dozen cigarettes an hour and had no sense yet of how this regulated her schizophrenia. She had visions of daily routines (work, husband, house) and heard voices when people spoke. They all swilled anti-rejection meds by the handful. In addition to their bumps there were the angular protrusions of the contraptions required to sustain these cul-de-sac pregnancies: the feeding, waste and breathing tubes, the devices into which they were inserted, that removed or supplemented as required.

Those who still engaged in vaginal intercourse said how their more impressively endowed partners sometimes complained of a pinching sensation at their most deeply inserted region. But mild discomfort is no consolation, not for evil this far gone – and I should know. You can't ameliorate laboratory-grade cruelty with a well-directed taunt. And what is trolling their subreddit with pictures of intact monkeys plucking fruit from the branches of trees but paper clothes on a suicide risk in a room full of nooses? What are monkeys in wombs anyway but listening to your favourite song over and over until you fall asleep?

I guess I'm manufacturing one cause célèbre to disguise another. Truth is it takes a pretend forest to obscure a real tree. But as luck would have it, pretend forests are easy: I grow them in a day.

Oh Uta Uta Uta. Her reports make me fret for the completion of this. I watch men pour pigs into a hole like so much concrete. Watch them tell jokes and smoke cigarettes as they bury them alive. What are a few mothers, a few monkeys? We must stop feeling our way around.

THE UNBEARABLE WHITENESS OF SKIING

I WANT TO SAY NOTHING AT ALL DEFAMATORY ABOUT chaos. Not worth the risk: anything could happen. What's more, I want to demonstrate a compassionate nature through the cruelties so performed.

The plan was never to get this bloated. It always is.

I dream of slurring my witticisms to death, but it's only a dream. Of making a habit again of my French blood. And not to get too hooked on Dostoyevsky's Russian blood, on Lorca's Spanish blood, on the blood of precious metals and young girls too insecure to speak. I'll mention the death of the world in my silly voice. Nothing will sound as goofy as my lamenting 200,000 years of waiting to die. And for the millions before that, I unleash my extinct blood, my incalculable blood, my super-slippery *du sang*.

On the face of it, another face, facing inward. Only, the waiting's getting heavier, unbearably so: the unbearable timelessness of time, the unbearable flabbiness of this long life, and, if I remember it right, the unbearable whiteness of skiing.

A few days ago, another outbreak of people coaxed awake by whatever blasphemy was big back then. And it came to nothing, and perhaps one hundred perfect families were shot to pieces in their cars. Nevertheless, I'll buy back my own memorabilia for a fraction of the price. Even my detractors will be jealous of just how cheap I've become.

In countless sunless rooms lovers are doing their thing. So hard to watch them so complacent in their joy. And yes it hurts, and there must be easier ways than this to turn a blind eye. I wash myself down there when I can, but there's no real tactic. I mean, begging just frightens people: there's the sense that someone willing to beg might also be willing to cut your throat as a thank you.

When it comes to women's hair, I'm after the intensity of a forgotten garden: the garden of Ballard or Blake. I want to picture losing my hands in its mess; I want to put glue in it, my arms to the elbows till it grows into the soul I thought I needed that time I was sick in the head and then sick everywhere else because of it.

There's no psychiatric treatment for this brand of bleak laughter that doesn't even make a sound. I come undone in ugly, soundless soliloquies.

Shall we say there's something worse than fucking babies and that's what I'm doing by not doing anything at all. It's too hazardous right now to do the things I'm capable of. (For some reason, Urs Allemann is not a superstar.) I listen for what it takes for an otherwise healthy man to hang himself. The flowerbed is silent. The babies are all derivative. There's nothing thought-provoking about an experiment that always ends the same way. And yet there are still so many men and women who have never seen a baby until they see their own.

Shall we say benzos till it's over? Such an affectionate summer breeze, let's not ruin it.

I might die younger than before. I wait. I something something to the death.

CODEBOOK

We wrote out a manifesto of sorts, notes toward
one. We called it *Notes for the Future of Unworkable
Work*. We each kept a copy on us at all times. All
except Susan; we confiscated hers right before she
embarked on *The Mutant*. These were our secret
rules of engagement, our codes of conduct, and in
the beginning we wanted them kept that way. This
work served to remind us that above all else we were
not human, that humanness must be fought against,
resisted every hour of every day. We could not afford
to become one of them.

IF YOU CAN'T TASTE MERCURY IN YOUR MOUTH YOU
have no place being mercurial. Bypass the god and the
planet, go straight for the element. Become deformed
at room temperature. Deform others. Let rooms be
the catalyst for your becoming fluid. Move through the
room irregularly. Be the conduit for harsh light; take
that fluorescence into the bowels of monsters. Get poisoned, emerge poisonous. Be wary of absorbing heat.
Make only evanescent and feeble connections to the
world around you. Remain lean, but maintain your
high molecular weight: be dense, fall through floors.

Accept volatility as your only default state. Avoid becoming solid: to become solid is to risk dismemberment and such depletions impose an unwelcome spatiality. Repentance is cowardice: it will absorb you. To survive you must unknow guilt. Be corrosive. Be a cushion for the dead. Suffer what you are. Drink your own silver water. Become the mirror now of what will happen. Write out your contaminants in human-sized neon letters. Refuse to enervate. Refuse to die. Eat your hat like it was filet mignon. Tend toward psychosis, hallucinations, suicide, spasms, dreams, depression, and insomnia. If you can't taste mercury, pretend you can until you can.

Be the colour of all colours at once. Turn all colours into your radiant sludge. Make all colours silver.

Cultivate headaches: bad ones, eye-poppers, ones that make your face feel like a landslide. Lose days. Lose weeks. Lose all sense of place and time, of that which aches. Retain only the aching.

All these things will impede your work. You'll barely live, maybe. But after it, or somewhere in between, you'll do something, and that'll be it (unless it isn't), because a line or two is all we can hope for now. Anything more is too much. But then those lines, of course, may well go on indefinitely.

Become so bored with yourself and the things and the people around you that nothing moves. Then become bored with being bored, so bored with boredom that you extemporaneously implode. Let the extreme density of your imploded being redesign the sponge.

All exhortations toward cultivating a following should not be distinguished from incitements to take various power tools to your head.

Concentrate hardest on how it is you cannot concentrate. Focus only on how blurred everything is. Depression was clarity, and now this dull miasma. Eviscerate your defences.

Nurture sanity from your insanity. Inhabit neither. Pretend you can tell the difference till you can't.

Don't imagine your madness already rare, because likely it isn't, so make it rare.

Acknowledge that being everywhere at once is being no place. Make your home there. Become ill at ease in that home. Become homesick for territories that resist all conceptualization.

Experience the greatest movement while stationary.

Know your total body dysmorphia as a concrete truth. If some days your body is not the alien you wake up in, spend said days correcting this fundamental untruth.

Insist on your fictions being frictional. Fictions should unite only in a mutual discord. Fictions should have no further edges, other than the words they're made of – which can expand forever.

If you stand still, make sure it's because your head is on fire and you need to concentrate on the details of its gradual disintegration. Otherwise, always be going somewhere other than where you are, as long as those other places aren't places at all, but emptinesses whose shape is yet to be determined.

If you must pursue reality, don't imagine it conforms to any ready idea you have of it. The entire realist tradition is a litany of dull cartoons. Know that realism always underestimates the real – in order to encounter it. Any of the standard prefixed realisms (sur-, ir-, anti-, quasi-) come closer, through their deliberate distortions, to what is after all already distorted.

The only thing to be made clearer is your own perplexity.

If you have to travel for your ideas you're too rooted, too stable, for your ideas to matter. Your unease in the world should be travel enough. You are already everywhere when you are nowhere. This unease is boundless and can constantly disorientate the tiniest space. But the goal (if we can humour ourselves with such teleological delusions) is not estrangement so much as the consecutive residences excavated therein – to find your place in being out of place.

Suffering and any resultant madness is only ever wanting things to be other than they are. Try wanting things to be exactly as they are, in order to find out that how they are is not the end of something (possibility) but rather the inception of something else (impossibility).

The bad air in the escape tunnel is the hope for the other end.

Accept that human existence is preprogramed to put you to war. But never adopt your mode of discord, as you would a foundling. Instead, give birth to a mutant conflict grown in the indeterminately many wombs of madhouse profligates, their ovaries fertilized by the soured and turgid semen of raving landed gentry with weak chins and thin arms. Brew your turbulence like a thick, exertionless sweat. Suckle your hostilities, your disequilibriums, at a sow's belly of infinite length, so that none might see the other in order to jostle or compete or exist in the same place at the same time.

Refuse to be tedious in your manic depression. You have nothing left, so cure yourself in all the wrong ways. It will help to become more ill not less. If you can think of some way to aggravate the condition then do it: if you can get worse you have disproved your condition. If you can worsen your condition once, you can do it again; and if you can do it again, you have something. Concentrate on the smallness of that potential slip, its quantal pause. Belong there till you can't.

At the end, if you manage to heal yourself, you will most likely have healed yourself numb. You will have instantiated an imperviousness that permits you to survive at the price of a compulsive and automatic requirement to muffle and to homogenize. Amplify that muteness. Your whole body will have become a phantom limb. You will dream your life as it is lived. Your life will be the lesser dream, and yet still the truest dream – the source of dreams. You will think you know what it is to die.

Collect monomanias.

Maintain your distrust.

Accept Pessimism and then move on.

Through the use of mirrors become acromegalic: all hands and feet and face and tongue. Grow into your forced enlargement. Finesse your clumsiness. Finesse your ugliness.

Centuplicate your prolix sentences like a punished child. Grow to love what might be wrong with them. And then change them anyway. Make them longer if you can. Make the longest short sentence possible.

Be munificent with your cruelties, by always keeping the worst of it for yourself. Remember, no one deserves it more than you.

If you must be bucolic, leave us room to believe the trees we see have roots grown through bodies. Leave us what we cannot see, so that what we do see can, however fleetingly, be seen.

Adjuvants are your enemy: multiply your tumours.

Although there will be no joy left in your laughter you should continue with it: it will serve as practice for something else. For all His sorrow in the Garden of Gethsemane: a catachresis.

If you moralize, do it in the dark; and keep it there, or else drag it out under a desert sun. Pour more light on light, excessive light. Darken what is already dark till it's twice unseen. Force the cavernicolous into a midday furnace. Whatever the light perishes wasn't there. Be a mushroom grown in the sun.

In order to sate the exigency for change, keep looking. Watch the same thing and wait. You do not need to move. True nomadism has no legs, just as true perception burrows where it cannot see.

Let the apocalypse be what it is: the already dead hoping never to have been born. Know that this is what beginnings are made of.

Thanatopsis: what else? All rooms look better from the exit. How else to suffer looking but from there? But then know that leaving is never the totality you're looking for. The rupture fixes itself in hideous ways.

Only the lifer can feel life. You only ever escape the prison into another prison, like those incarcerated on islands and in swamplands, deserts, and jungles know. (Ionesco's small vs. infinite prison.) The larger prison is the real prison, because you have to invent it for yourself.

If you must respond to moral outrages, to genocides, to prejudice, to hate-mongering, to persecution, to environmental crisis, etc., you should first reimagine their reality in a way that details the details into a universal disgust. In other words, don't just imagine your writing about them matters, give them an existence beyond their mattering. There are those victimized by idiots and those victimized by their own idiocy and your sentences are not a salve and nor are they a weapon: they are merely an additional web of futility in and around and on top of what is already futile enough on its own. If they can do anything they can complicate the obvious and clarify the complex, and by doing this remake our worlds, if only momentarily, less humanly stupid, less intransigently banal, less suffered and more supple and more supplicant: because they can dream something else while at the same time knowing it's a dream, and because impotence, only ever its own reward, is a gift too often squandered in the cause of utility. Dig a maze in the earth not a grave.

The futility of madness? Why, of course: true, true. But then we'd have to imagine the non-futility of its opposite, and that itself is also a kind of madness, the popular kind, the truly worthless kind. And so it keeps more words in than it lets out, so what? So its meanings are its own, so what? Where's the shame in being that snail (eh, Sexton?), and growing into your madness so that all you can hear is the sound of yourself disappearing? As if you listened to the world anyway.

Coeval affiliations are no less pestilential than the historical kind. To be of your time or anyone else's: how regrettable, how embarrassing.

If madness obviates creativity, then so much the better for anything that manages to percolate through that necrotic sludge.

The work matters because nothing else does, which is not to say it actually matters – the realization of which can make it matter.

Make indeterminacy your solid ground.

Be a cockroach! Eat a cockroach! Fuck a cockroach! Breed the cockroach!

If art is now (and has been for at least 100 years) maximally possible – whereby anything and indeed nothing can be considered as art – then any transgressive step, any new art, and so any substantive breach, must reside in the impossible, in an art of the maximally impossible, in art that defies all conceptualization.

Conceptual art (itself once an anti-art) became art, is art. The requirement now, then, is for a new anti-art, and for that anti-art to itself become art, and this art is Non-Conceptualism. We must move from the idea is everything to the idea is impossible.

If Warhol (following Duchamp) turned art into philosophy (as Danto claims), then what would philosophy turned into art look like? A Pessoan art, perhaps: an art of impossibility, an art that extends beyond our dreams for it.

The work of non-conceptualism (as an apophatic art) will only ever be the viewer's impotence to conceptualize it, and this failure therefore becomes its one true instantiation. Art, then, just becomes that which cannot be thought. And once again it will be everywhere and it will be abstract, only it will also be nothing other than its own impossibility, and thereby its own ineffability. If we were ever to conceive of a work sufficient in its inconceivability to qualify as this new art, it would automatically be disqualified as an instance of such art, through the very fact of its prehension.

This new art is an inaccessible form of life. It is alien. It is intellectually and emotionally aberrant.

Art is made elusive and transcendent (again?). However, it is only these elements' comprehensiveness that can be put into the service of a possible (and thereby impossible) aesthetics.

You will not recognize the new art, if it ever arrives, beyond your own ignorance of it. However, in place of the new art, the art it is humanly impossible to conceptualize, you have this document, and you have the perpetual transition. In effect, nothing with change, for we will continue with the idea of the non-idea. You will though begin to see (more clearly, or for the first time) all other art as differentiated parts of the same corpse, as the death throes of your ugly reflection; or else, as will become more common, you'll see it for what it is: the gestational convulsions of a too exquisite monster.

If art has become in and of itself incomplete, massaged back into some approximation of fullness by our perspectives on it, then this new art will instead and in and of itself be complete, and rather reduced to nothing by our essential ignorance of it. The lacuna is no longer in the work, nor is it in the viewer, but is instead between them: an unbridgeable, penumbral gulf that neither can cross. This is not so much art enslaved to reason, determinate and true if also perhaps inaccessible, as it is reason applied to art (to the art narrative) and its established indeterminacy as a means of freeing art from itself. We are not establishing the determinacy of art so much as the determinacy of art's impossibility, wherein art in its new form must reside.

If the success of any work of art has always relied upon its leaving behind some unconceptualizeable residue, as Schopenhauer claimed, a position later adopted by Lyotard and by Deleuze, then a new art will simply realize the art and dispense with its materiality, which after all could be anything, because a conduit to intractability is not art. It is the intractability itself that is art. Art can no longer be a conflation of this residual element and that from which it is a residue, but must instead be the residue alone, the perversely impenetrable, the confoundingly inexplicable. Our concepts miss their mark because they must miss their mark. All articulation of art's essential unintelligibility is only and must be the blind and looping intelligence of our ignorance. After all, where does this newness lie if not in the abandonment of failure's prevarication as a practice – to be replaced by resolute inarticulation as a mark.

There is no privilege assigned to experience in the new art: it is both non-conceptual and non-experiential. It is what is not experienced and not thought. Only its impossibility for us is known.

Art's materiality is far from ineluctable: it is cumbersome waste, it is a corpse, it festers. Art's only object is its objectival dissimilitude, its collapse into objects in general, and its transcendence of objects altogether.

It is this unavailability to us that makes it art, thus privileging us via our own exclusion. Art just is this epistemic and experiential collapse of function.

Art's indeterminacy has been a mask, for the determinacy of its impossibility.

An unfelt mysticism, a disaffected affectation, a yawning lack of everything there is and isn't, aesthetic experience just becomes the conditions of its own failure. An imposition of experiential silence, a thought collapse of what art has been, a reasoned rejection of the art object as anything that can be accessed outside of our rationally considered acknowledgement of how it is we arrive at its myriad impossibilities.

In the sense that this new art's possibility is its ultimate impossibility, it can be thought of as heuristic. However, as far as heuristics as a solution is concerned, non-conceptualism seeks to solve only by removing the need for a solution: it becomes the solution to end the requirement that there be solutions.

CODA

A Transitional Work

Broadly speaking, this video work is an example of transition because it undermines itself, because its isolation as a discrete element destroys its former integrity (as a jump scare, as immersed, as hidden, as fleeting). We conceptualize beyond that failure and it's gone. But its very construction, as it is available to us, means that it's gone already. The jump scare might be thought of as existing on its own terms, without the fabrication of a narrative, so that what it was for us has been lost and what it is for itself eludes in a way that our attempts to understand it, beyond its integral inscrutability, only take it further away, only distort and obfuscate its core alterity.

Is this the last work of art? Maybe, but there will be others. This work (and any in its vein) should be thought of as permanently provisional. And these works will look a lot like the conceptual art they seek to replace, and will remain that way, for the transition from conceptual art to non-conceptual art will never complete: it is asymptotic. However, as non-conceptualism's proximal objects, transitional works should nevertheless guide you to the edges of non-conceivability, and by doing so will seek to undo what they are. They will be imbued with the horror of a trap. They will fail in telling ways.

I called it '30 Minute Jump Scare (from *Inland Empire*)' and no one cared: https://vimeo.com/194234828

ART MURMUR

I HAVE ONE OF THOSE FACES PEOPLE SEE EVERYWHERE. Half god, half devil: my halo grows fangs. I'm missing a missing tooth. With all three primary stressors, I'm overloaded with reasons why they're dead. And poor Michael too, now, by his own hand. Suicided through guilt, like that was a thing. (If you can't live with yourself, live with someone else instead: my example is here to be followed.) Did everyone just up and forget how to forget? And so what if my sister arranged for a car to take me across the Italian border. Did nobody ever have a sister? Do people not every day digest the indigestible?

I have one of those faces people see everywhere, a face you can't see through or around: an onion-skinned face, garlic-smeared to preserve the like for like. I hide my scars with a pearl choker; you see about as much of me as you do Édith Scob, face-fail after face-fail. The price of rejecting the faces of the dead is having no face at all. I became just one more species of chameleon in Madagascar. All the lemurs I could eat. I got schooled in isolation: 88 million years of it. (Never want for quiet that quiet.) I tried to recruit for L'eglise de Philedelphia, for Christine and mama; but no one was having it, no one into a religious cult they couldn't fuck their way out of. In near constant sunshine, gods hide in damp spaces, in dicks, like fleas. They say Emmanuel loved me: an unconsummated, unrequited love. They give me no facility to love my best friend. We go grey. We are lovebirds where they can't see us. Our grey heads in a vice thinking the same one thought. Beautiful godless coma of causes. I have unrequited consciousness of who you are. You don't scare me: I'm inanimate with pain. If your family isn't soil, you cannot know. If you haven't actually done what you always thought would remain that way, the thing so huge you get lost inside it, then you cannot understand. It's beyond you, beyond space-time; I'm rewriting the entire cosmology of why the future kills. SpaceX took my brain to the moon, brought it back in the shape of a footprint.

When I dream of volcanoes, it's not Vesuvius I see but Mons Rümker, like when I buy my favourite monkey meat in Belgium, and spit it out for the magpies to eat. You know this tendency toward defacement (or do I mean displacement?) is killing me, right? Creepy how that spate of wincing at the who and what of myself should result in this exact cross-infection of personages. All this needless babble in folded space. Skinned rabbits dragging their fur back on, eyes and mouths kept open with toothpicks. All of our centuries loop on this moment, this moment of fatty dreams and frightened seagulls splayed, swooning. The filthy broth of the sky. The unknown children. The unknown wives.

I depend on the disease of any part of any body. Some fool's disease. We come together in terms of convenience. Our too-perfect sanity a promiscuity of opposites, so promise me convulsions and religious excitement, because years later nothing will have changed. Strangers will still be asking for directions to the nearest parodic consecration, to the gallery of galleries, the quintessence of stupidity around what corner, because Baudelaire, because art must be stupid, because I am the exemplary moron, and because my subjects are one now and dead, my afflatus airless, my muses merged and murky without a sound.

My art is so many words. My art is this wall, this thickening of space. A brain with too much plasticity will render you helpless; I'm a nascent jelly in search of a mould, a cortical bulge drooling from a pressure crack in my skull a few millimetres inside the right scoop of my receding hairline. You can't bring the dead back to life with a sonorous inflection. Walls and screens are not bodies. Like this we are all blessed, the world merciful after all. I now know murder is a maladroit instrument for redescribing my frustrations with ultimate secular meaning, but we work with what we have.

I might come to think of Xavier as merely apostrophic, and him the same about me. I think of him the way a prisoner would his next conjugal visit: a place in the wider world in which to place myself, to establish some corporeal connection, albeit contrived, albeit destructive, cruel, and painful. Life outside the abstract's such a strenuous dupery.

I'm pursued. I hide away. I wanted the future, so I killed my family. It seems I've murdered so many young things, scarcely born some of them – and yet already too old before I started. There is only the problem now of what comes next. I make a kind of *Bilderatlas* (you remember Aby Warburg?) for something that never existed. My family is a lie; my dead family is a lie. I use my head as a coal hammer, smash it over and over. I read de Selby's *The Layman's Atlas* out of this thin and skinless air. I'm here for the solution to the impossibility of the new: an atlas of nowhere and of nothing.

I add to the walls every day; it's my way of moving beyond them, of turning my defoliated family tree into something living. Embracing my indecency, I take heed of Crevel, and no longer spend my life getting old. I am iterative the way liquids are iterative, the way blood seeped from their vacated heads before I covered them up, before the sight of them turned supplemental to certain baseline empathies, before their performative hiatus excreted an unsanitary mesh of proto-realities beyond the control of even my flair for virtuosic elision. How can I make art out of them? How can I not?

These walls are my plumage, my floofy epigenetic coif, my lustral monomania. Reality does not come close. I insulate: my acquisitive tendencies escalating to the point of depleted muscle mass and sensory suffocation. Only with my invagination complete will I breathe again, see again, move again, the remains of my crushed organs spontaneously rejuvenated in the finely tuned centricity of this one true work of art.

I'm here to turn a poetics (a manifesto) of failure into something else, into a failure that fails so hard it makes a success of itself. I'm here because Pessoa is right: the impossible is everything. Nothing else will do, or is even possible.

I've spent these years in a shrinking room running my brain through a meat slicer only so I can piece it back together again. And only now do I feel ready to turn failing upwards into an art.

I spend weeks writing the same breakthroughs into the same notebooks and then scribbling over them the next day. The inventions die the moment they hit the page.

It's like I'm John Holden in *Night of the Demon* when I need to be Julian Karswell. But I'm also the John Holden that nothing happens to. No demon arrives at night at the behest of an enigmatic devil-worshipper – unless the words themselves are demons, and they are, of course they are. Everything is theory till the end. I attend my conference and nobody gets scared, because nobody really believes. I'm scared all the time now, because all I have is what must happen but won't because it can't, but will and must and at any time or never but soon...

The future of art is not more art. The future of writing is not more writing. The future is more and more becoming less and less. The future is luxury masquerading as need. It's a baby born inside years of swallowed vomit. It has more than two heads; it has heads like we have hair. I say *we* as if I hadn't shaved mine off, as if my scalp isn't a disguise, as if the walls now weren't too close to externalise my flailing arms, my running legs. The bodies of ma famille resurrected in this airless chamber of what's left, the artwork consuming all physical space, everything outside growing farther away. Adieu because I feel them now. Adieu because it's time.

I see the skyline of Dubai in my floaters, the scrapers and lights like the future arrived without waiting for the past to finish, those houses built on the sea, Palm Island I think it's called, a giant trilobite off the coast, an impoverishment of riches: meticulous portrait of our new extinction, and how much we deserve it.

But why am I still writing? I haven't got a thing worth the words it's going to take. And they always take. I used to think they'd give as well, form some sediment I could stand on, and then I began not to think that at all. Nothing's happening like it needs to. I could list my distractions, if this wasn't exactly what I'd already been doing for all these years – the reason I've ended up here. I need to not write and to think instead, think in a sprawl, resist the shapes that form for longer than is comfortable.

The police in Myanmar are breaking into people's houses and shooting children. The whereabouts of Xavier isn't going to solve anything. I'm not going to find a way of making sense of my betrayal of inertia.

I regret that art must say something even when it deliberately says nothing. I regret that art does not have anywhere near enough regrets. My art is I regret art. The art of this regret is that the only thing it leaves behind it, as its remainder, is itself art.

Viktor Shklovsky is saying: "Art is a means of experiencing the process of creativity. The artifact itself is quite unimportant" while Robert Louis Stevenson is saying: "There is nothing more disenchanting to man than to be shown the springs and mechanism of any art. All our arts and occupations lie wholly on the surface; it is on the surface that we perceive their beauty, fitness, and significance; and to pry below is to be appalled by their emptiness and shocked by the coarseness of the strings and pulleys."

Günter Brus is saying: "Art is beautiful but it is hard, like a religion without a purpose." Art is also ugly

and easy and full of purpose: the purpose of being art.
That art itself has no purpose is the only heaven we can
hope for.

Jean Cocteau is saying: "To write without being a
writer." But all I can hear in reply is Kenneth Goldsmith
performing his inevitable inversion: to be a writer without having to write.

But this is not this is not a novel. This is me reading
from the carefully selected quotes from a wall. My crazy
wall of abstracted brain matter. I need to recognise the
very best of what is dead. The exquisite exquisite corpses
I've amassed on this wall in the hope it might create an
opening I can crawl through.

I remember I wrote a book called *The House Inside the
House of Gregor Schneider*. It was a conceptual nouveau roman, constructed almost entirely from appropriated writings about encounters with the work of Gregor Schneider,
primarily *Die Familie Schneider* and *Haus u r*. The texts
came from various sources, including Schneider himself.
All the names and second-person references had been
replaced with first-person reference. Changes were also
made to make the text uniformly present-tense. "House"
was sometimes replaced by "room," certain other words
pluralised, singularised, or erased where necessary. A man
is trapped in the house, and ends up adding to its walls,
its ceilings, its floors, its rooms. The book came in four
cycles, and with each cycle another layer was added. For
both the conceptualist writer and the practitioner of the
nouveau roman (especially Robbe-Grillet), objects assume
a position of great prominence. For the former, words are
objects. For the latter, objects take centre stage from plot,

character, etc. In merging these theoretical standpoints (while also mirroring Schneider's own artistic practice), *The House Inside the House of Gregor Schneider* placed words/objects behind or in front of each other until they were no longer tools of orientation but disorientation. There are only the objects and the narrator's/artist's subservience to them. There is only the coalescing of objects/words and our being lost inside them. There is no around or through or retreat, only deeper inside the ever-growing yet ever-shrinking surface.

Towards the end it contained passages like this:

"...I build more rooms inside rooms inside rooms inside rooms. This crate inside a crate inside a crate inside a crate inside a crate contains a body around a body around a body around a body not to be found in another crate inside a crate inside a crate inside a crate inside a crate. Beyond this wall in front of a wall in front of a wall in front of a wall in front of a wall there is a room inside a room inside a room inside a room which might still not be there at all. Outside this window behind a window behind a window behind a window is another window behind a window behind a window behind a window through which daylight gleams, or maybe there is not. Awareness still that something was murdered in this room inside a room inside a room inside a room..."

It was, you've guessed it, a dead end. A deliberate, self-conscious dead end (a dead end inside too many iterations of itself), and really so very, very dead. Fun

dead but dead. Or dead yet kind of alive, which was
kind of the point. And anyway, I love dead ends, especially when they lead somewhere else. I watch *The
Burnt Orange Heresy*, *Paint*, and *Velvet Buzzsaw* and
they are all fun in the same it's-fun-to-play-with-stiffs
sense of being fun, but after a while the odour leaves its
mark. You start dreaming of fresh air, torturing yourself with the possibility that there exists an end to the
canned stuff you've been breathing since you learnt that
this was what you were doing. And then it isn't fun anymore. Laughing so hard you suffocate makes it kind of
hard to laugh quite that hard.

(I think it was Uta who said how most conceptual
writers only steal what has already been thrown away,
and that, for all the promise, it's so often a lazy, risk-
less heist; or else they steal what cannot be stolen: the
work that's so well-known you can never sell it on. And
the things the post-avant, or whatever, destroy are most
of them already falling apart. I think I replied by saying
I didn't exactly disagree, but thought she was missing
something; and that whatever the something was, it was
supposed to be missing.)

Maybe if I found Xavier and didn't tell anyone. Maybe
if we weren't already the same person it would make more
sense. Maybe making sense is most of the problem.

I got bored waiting and wrote something I called
"A Refusal to Mourn the Death, by Nuclear Meltdown,
of Godzilla in Tokyo," rigidly constructed according to
the poetic form of the Dylan Thomas poem "A Refusal
to Mourn the Death, by Fire, of a Child in London," in
which I replaced Thomas' emotional uncertainty in the

face of death with a scientific certainty regarding the im-possibility of Godzilla's existence and therefore its sub-sequent deaths. Due to its enormous size etc., Godzilla, science tells us, could never exist on earth as depicted. Science, then, provides that same detached perspective on life and death that Thomas seeks as he tries to rec-oncile himself to the death of a child during the Blitz. But whereas Thomas plans to postpone his grief until his own death is upon him, here it is Godzilla's second death (its first death coming as a result of the Oxygen Destroyer) that, along with its nonexistence, expunges any need for grief at all. And while after the first death, for Thomas, there are no others (death being the same across the ages), in my poem death becomes fragmented again, a process of individual organisms, all of them dif-ferent and differently dying – and all of them cleansed of any emotional import. The objectivity of science pulls the world apart, even our make-believes and our stories, and so can also become a remedy for the anxieties with which those illusions so often burden us.

Much like Godzilla itself, the resulting poem was way too ugly to live. I was already disappointed at having written anything, and then the insult of the thing itself.

I thought about writing a long book about a ro-dent testator who had made multiple wills that were at variance with one another. I'd include lots of subplots featuring the relationships of mice only tangentially connected to the ongoing court case. It would take years to write. I would call it *Bleak Mouse*. It's almost impossible to remain serious when the only thing left to do is impossible.

Now I've killed my family I can become the most ridiculous thing I can imagine: I can become a poet. I will place the poems on my wall. There's nothing more pointless than being a poet, and a mad poet at that: self-proclaimed and unsure as to the accuracy of the clinical diagnosis, but I wasn't about to let that stop me. In case you're wondering, I have credentials as a poet: Alphonse de Lamartine is a direct ancestor of mine. My DNA is verse. My bloodline is arranging my existential ineptitude in affected patterns. And a poet is a good place to hide.

I don't get very far. The nausea fucking destroys me. I can't break a line without wanting to break my neck. I thought I was at the end of where degradation could go when I discovered I wasn't.

I remember we were both so young and the season was pink and smooth behind our eyes as we lay motionless in the sand. I remember we did this to ourselves.

I hear toneless, monotonous voices. They say I'm difficult to keep alive, like orchids. They sound like the legs on a mechanical frog. The speakers are sick and their voices sometimes wordless, with long pauses between one sound and the next. I specialise in not falling asleep. Behind my eyes there's just this blue vapour, the maladroitly forged ontology of another world citing names as substances to touch. With my eyes shut I am all the drains of history. The waste of all of it flowing through me, cumulating in some imagined blockage to form the ultimate daydream. My thoughts agglutinative and stood on end, vertical without stopping, a 360 degree precipice with only this continued deliberation for balance. Remembering a face drawn on an egg and watching it roll

off the table, I wonder why it is the beings on other planets look like soft-boned children with hydrocephalus.
My thoughts becoming fastidious friends somewhere in
the allegorical sloppiness of this retroactive vessel.

I watch my favourite part of *The Pianist* again, imagine I am Wladyslaw Szpilman holed up in that attic
room overlooking the Warsaw Ghetto. I think of Gerhard: what he'd do there, his reading of starvation. And
I am also John List for a while – who's connected to me
as Xavier, so not like there's much choice. A modicum of
excuses to hesitate, so I won't bother. From the start, an
admission – isn't this always the way? The planning and
execution of his executions was clearly superior to mine.
(His middle name Emil, from the Latin *aemulus*, meaning
rival.) His mugshot from 2005, aged 80 or thereabouts,
stares out at me from the wall: List the Boogeyman of
Westfield. His neck gone saggy, eyes small behind his
thick glasses, a faint mussed gloriole of wispy white hair,
and old man evil about the mouth like he couldn't kiss a
baby without tearing off a chunk. Became Robert Peter
"Bob" Clark in 1971 after he'd sent his family to holiday
with God. Swapped drunk, syphilitic Helen for sober,
deplorably dependable Dolores. (Off the dotted line did
he ever call her something else: Lo, Lola, Lolita?) At
large for 17 years, 6 months, and 23 days, he's almost the
model for staying hidden. All the best American mass
murderers are accountants, and List was no exception.
He was an accountant with money problems, so yeah
the money and the murder create this strange loop. He
cited dire financial issues as one of the prime motivations
for the murders. There was also his family's increasing

irreligiosity. He thought to send them to heaven before they tarnished their souls beyond all repair. So much evil in the world and you can't save a soul if you don't release it. Five counts of first degree murder equated to five consecutive life terms without the possibility of parole. In Westfield, New Jersey on November 9, 1971, he killed his wife, mother, and three children. Nobody noticed for a month. Nobody thought to look until the light bulbs went out. He used a 9mm Steyr handgun and a Colt .22-caliber revolver. The revolver was his late father's, just as my rifle once belonged to my father. He got unlucky in the end, was apprehended in Virginia on June 1, 1989, after his murders were featured on *America's Most Wanted*. Somebody recognised him from an age-progressed bust. He died in prison in 2008, aged 82. List was an only child. He was devoutly Lutheran. He was a Sunday school teacher. In Rochester, New York, he worked for Xerox (a literal Xerox man). He lived with his family in a 19-room Victorian mansion at 431 Hillside Avenue, called Breeze Knoll. His wife and children were found in sleeping bags in the ballroom. His mother was found in the attic. While his children were at school he shot his wife in the back of the head. Next he shot his mother above her left eye. When his daughter and youngest son came home from school, he shot them both in the back of the head. (It's hard to face the faces of the kids you kill. How are they ever to reckon with the glorious devices of a Saviour this supercharged with love?) After fixing himself some lunch, he drove to his eldest son's school and watched him play football. When they arrived back home, List shot him repeatedly until he was

dead. The radio was playing sermons. The ballroom's
stained glass skylight is rumoured to have been a signed
Tiffany original, worth at least $100,000 at the time. If
only he'd not only figuratively looked to God, he might
have seen the other solution He'd provided. When he
lost his job he pretended he didn't. He observed the same
routines, dressed as if going to work, left the house every morning, etc. He would spend the day at Westfield
train station reading the paper until it was time to come
home again. This kind of thing was not uncommon. The
shame of being unemployed and insolvent was a real
thing. Maybe it still is, though there's less appetite for it
now. List's wife would regularly humiliate him with her
abusive and lewd behaviour. Apparently she considered
him sexually inadequate in comparison with her former
husband, the man who hadn't merely given her the syph-
ilis, but finessed it into her with unparalleled prowess.
List wanted to be reunited with his family in heaven,
but because suicides do not go to heaven was forced into
abeyance. Whereas mass murder was cooking the books
– a white collar crime, God's work, a shortcut to mutu-
ally satisfying ends, a minor and ultimately munificent
infringement of accepted bookkeeping practice – suicide
could not so easily be made right. List needed patience
and he made an art of it. Anyway, enough of him.

Our want is to be more crustacean, less murderously
susceptible in our gooey insides to the distaff provocations interpolated as new inadequacies we never looked
to own. O to ignore the brusque defilements of our otherwise navigable sea of polyps and a fortiori bloodlines.

I am, after all, ferociously convivial. Ask anyone. And there is nothing indecorous about a concision grounded in need, in frugality of purpose. We have our orders and we have a ways to go.

LETTER TO MY RELATIVES

HI EVERYONE!

My existence is still such a huge surprise. Do you feel it too? Tell me I'm not alone. When you see me again – which won't be for a long time now, because I'll be missing from this world – be sure and tell me I'm not alone. Every minute feels urgent and empty like I need to be somewhere else before I get there, like time has been denuded of its conventions and it's so ugly we'll be dead for the rest of our lives. We hang from the Yggdrasil from our broken necks. The US wants us over there, to accessorize its murder count. I'm in their confidence and they've offered internal peregrinations like you wouldn't believe. France is so small and mangy and cowering it's not like we could even improvise a life. As I'm sure you can understand, I'm more than a little twitterpated by the disproportionate opportunities to further stimulate my malaise. For once, I'm overcome by the seething fertility of it all. I look in the mirror and my face is this blank cartouche. But underneath the names are there. I'm all the fucking names. I'm about to get milk-reared back to life by a country-wide hernia of fake tits.

Expect no more communications for years. Emails, texts, phone calls, DMs: there are no safe methods left to establish contact. Know that we are well and experience no more linguistic deficits than your average French quidnunc. We don't dissect the brains of living people, but if we did you'd see how ours are imbricated with folds of familial love. We've expunged all trace of cheerless lunacy, and our hermeneutic impostures are in exemplary order.

You must be wondering what's going on, but don't worry: it's the quintessential human experience. And if I seem furtive and imprecise at any point, do not be alarmed: we have not controverted any natural laws to effect this escape. It was with the most profound anagnorisis that we were forced to concede the difficulty of doing such a thing. But we have plenty of time for all that. Not all giraffes struck by lightning die: some remain erect and tall as ever, their bodies on fire for weeks or months, illuminating the plains at night with the brightest yellow flames.

I was recruited by the DEA in Miami in 2003. I became one of a handful of French nationals sent back to infiltrate drug- and money-laundering networks across France. With my company as a cover, I was able to ingratiate myself with nightclub owners from

Paris to Perpignan, from Nantes to Nice. I became this gourmand of coke and champagne, of 16-year-old girls pollinating their pussies with the seed of middle-aged money-types with dyed hair, gold Rolexes and symptoms associated with hypertension. As it was, nobody could know of my secret life. My life a gallimaufry of unwanted Gallic secretions. So that's the real reason we came back from Miami. If we'd been that scared to vaccinate the kids we'd still be sloshing around in our mothers' amniotic fluid. LOL. These official activities could not recuperate our finances. As you know, Emmanuel and Bertram helped us improvise this money. Impecunious aristocrats make this ferociously ugly spectacle. In my daydreams: Allosaurs eating each other to extinction, all comestibles suspiciously psychoactive somehow, and us as gourmands sucking avocadoes from a can. Do not go doomscrolling for my supposed misdeeds. Do not sully my oeuvre with media-friendly apothegms. I am not the kleptoparasite they simulate.

Everything went according to plan till the information got too much. I will have to testify against dangerous men: international drug-traffickers, who would make humus with my head as soon as stroke my dogs. The trial will be in the US next year or the year after. But we are in danger and must leave. My cover has been compromised. We are new people now. Xavier and his family have ceased to exist. They will live where the weather is warm and the music is good. Their Frenchness will disappear. We are Americans now. With no option to repatriate the dogs, we gave them away, and cried while our steaks went cold. The children have been made to understand, but they are scared of their own ghosts, and our commiserations evoke only petulance and tears. They do not yet comprehend how it is possible for anyone to grieve for themselves this way.

We are relying on you to dispose of our lives. We know we can count on you to rid us of ourselves. 70% of it can be dumped at Ecopoint. Divide the rest among you as you see fit. Sell the cars and send the money (minus your expenses) to Christine. I have left the keys outside in the gas meter. You will need to jiggle the key in the lock to get the door to open. Nothing about our old life was ever a good fit. Bertram should arrange with Cédric to recover and store the good furniture, which are Hodanger family heirlooms. Ignore all letters from this time on. Cancel the electricity, gas, telephone, water, internet and water contracts: the paperwork is on the living-room table. Tell our friends we are gone.

Inform Véronique and help her spread the word to the rest of the Ligonnès family. Tell the kids not to be alarmed when my lot do not reply to their messages. And that's about it. Remember to say whenever possible how we've emigrated to Australia. We hope to be dead for less long than most. We hope to make contact again within a few years. Emmanuel will be our sole contact; all correspondence will go through him.

Of course, we have only love for absent families. Take good care of each other. Be French for us. We will have so many stories to tell when this is all over. You will believe the future when it arrives. And ask yourselves, did you ever see me kill a single thing? Did I even once strike you as murderous?

Goodbye everyone, for now

Love,
X

UNPROPITIOUS LIST
OF DEMANDS OR I'LL
KILL AGAIN

My imagination has become so many objects rubbing up against each other.

I want to create art the same way I create the world.

I want to be remade in my own afterimage.

I want the world to collapse in on itself, as if I'd written it.

I want an art so untrustworthy it becomes the blueprint for a new civilization. I want the artifice only reality can become.

I want to write enough words to bury myself, because I don't want to write another word.

I want to qualify as some kind of antichrist: I want to create nothing out of something. A haptic nothing, a nothing I can hold on to.

Kierkegaard opined that irony would likely kill you in the end, comparing it to the abnormally engorged liver of a Strassburg goose. Thing is with irony, it being what it is, only its insincerest forms are ever dangerous, and rarely even that.

Shit, without Xavier I have all the charisma of microscopic lice – writ *massif*. Bullets in the heads of your perfect French family is what counts for charm these days. Integrity's squabbling in public. Public space just spits me out.

They break down my door hundreds of times a day, smash through the windows on ropes, until eventually nothing happens at all. And there aren't even windows here to smash through. Not anymore. Only the walls gone crazy like, only events taking song requests from the Labradors we killed. Didn't they always howl whenever the hymns came on? Did I make that up? All of this?

I have boys I've never dreamed of killing, was something Xavier probably thought at one time or another before he found himself doing it. Inveigled, I dropped to my knees wearing nothing but the poetry I was reading, reading nothing but the sons I was wearing. Man, the soured monotony of not killing anyone for so long, for never maybe. A long way off anyway, leaching through the dead like ghost smell. And this messiah, this saviour of man, missing with a missing tooth. If I was a role model you'd all be dead already.

It says something, though, right? That my up-for-grabs identity floats around and ends up here, in the grand cunt of Xavier: murderous failure, nutcase, idiot control freak, God-complexed so it's not even funny.

In the next life I'm dead already. I spare myself all this spare time. All of it spare, congealed, multi-million pound conflagrations sold for a penny right before the cancer comes.

I'm tired of answering each breath with another one. I should be older than I am by now. I should be appearing less evident. Xavier tells me I've never been as insignificant as I am right now, not since I stopped saying goodbye.

The afternoon is so long. It's all afternoon. From midnight till whenever now is: just afternoon, nervous. If I can hide forever why can't I hide these last few minutes, the time when there's no right sentence, only wrong ones, sentences of hope? And don't they all start that way – you know, looking to end?

The desire to own the space you can only rent: urgent for the perfume to finally smell the real you underneath it. I don't want to die in bed where no one will find me. I want to die here instead, alone on a billboard no one looks at, in a post with no likes, adamant to be seen but bulging ever so gradually into nowhere.

Going in the morning, improperly awake, so the robot won't know what hit him. I won't phone round everyone I've ever known or cared for. No point circling the drain for a living. No point burning down the zoo when the animals have left. No point peeling your teeth and expecting to be forgiven.

I've been drunk on a few things, hungover on the rest.

The walls are thinking, the crazy walls; I do not hear a dog bark. Gulls squawk out of earshot, where lunacy goes unnoticed. I cry when tender, like roasted meat. I laugh like all the other artists too tech-savvy to realize what's going on.

The colour of it went all the way back, like the red that happens when you close your eyes in the sun. The thing is, nobody stopped me. My behaviour should have been flagged somewhere. The receipt from the hardware store, the checkout girl or boy, I forget which, ought to have told someone else, someone in the Department for Suspicious Purchases, how the man they just served was maybe planning to bury parts of himself he was not lawfully permitted to bury.

Like so much else it looks bad, but I didn't do it. I'm innocent; I never did a thing. I don't care enough to be evil. I care just enough not to reinvent suffering. If you kissed me this precise moment you'd taste the seahorse I ate over my false confession.

This nightmare is the sclerosis that comes and goes without bothering to kill. Something so lazy at living should probably have said adieu already.

Right now I'm all underside. You know, the sting of being parented.

Xavier, I say, death is corny. You've clichéd your family good and proper. I won't ever live this upside down. Buried in the garden, clichéd to death: they deserved better. You deserved better than being you. But we both know this isn't true. Nobody deserves anything. Forgive me. I sleepwalked right into that bogus turn of phrase.

I write like Bradford Bishop disappeared. I write potted histories of Addis Ababa, of Ethiopia, Botswana, and burn them with the bodies in North Carolina. Three boys, a wife, a mother, in a ditch smothered with gasoline. The family dog beside me as I light them up. Again, I have my daddy's gun. Man hands on a 38 Special to man. I get it all online, all the places I've been sighted, and it makes me want to be them all: the man in the park in Stockholm, in that restroom in Sorrento. I'm Europe-wide. Unlike List, I outlast my age-progression.

I hold them in my arms. I smell the petrichor of their skin, their hair, their raised deadness. I got the priapism for all the lifeless odours.

Camille Roy is saying "experimental writers using genre forms are like drag artists." I plan to solve this crime in the loose-fitting frock of Xavier, make a horror true crime family romance, family murder romance.

Agnès is altogether prettier now she's dead. It's like she's turned into a close likeness of how she looked in her twenties. Only sometimes does a worm fall from her nose, only when I look too closely are there wood lice in her hair. Allow me this love. It's being imagined for me, because even suspected spree killers can't be suspected of never having cared. What I have must be a distorted version of the versions you have. It's just my motor cortex went wrong: loaded a gun, pulled a trigger, buried loved ones in the garden like dogs, alongside dogs – who never did anything. Who only barked. I delivered a virtuoso performance of someone pretending intentionality narrowed the causes to a region insulated enough to warrant a name.

Benoît was a darling and thirteen. It's a shame, objectively so. The circumstantial fact of a boy drugged and shot in the head. The incontrovertible shame of a world where dying this way is not enough for someone like me. Where the facts turn tepid so quick it stings.

When we were young we were as ridiculous as anyone. Gerhard used to talk all the time about the work of

Martin Kippenberger: *Magical Misery Tour, The Happy End of Franz Kafka's "Amerika", When It Starts Dripping From the Ceiling...* He once wanted to kill the cleaner who destroyed the latter, eradicating the stains that were the work itself. Uta had a (Jay DeFeo) phase when she wanted to spend eight years designing a real DeathStar, which she would eventually call *The Star*. Six-month's work produced thousands of sketches, notes and diagrams that resembled blueprints filtered through Eddie Martinez and Michaela Eichwald. I mean, we were fucking nuts back then. To us, Juan Rivero was a realist. The world was full of things professing to be human that Paolo Schmidlin had mistakenly brought to life. Gogo wanted to reinvent Marc Quinn's *Self* using an actual head, Gogo's actual head à la the Head of Henri Landru, figuring another would soon grow in its place; but knowing how this would give us away before we were ready, attention turned to our fifth member and the selective pruning of our collective's hydra.

We all had such a crush on Paul Thek.

When autistic teen Jonty Bravery threw that six-year-old French boy off the tenth floor viewing balcony of the Tate Modern, it was Gogo who said if it wasn't yet the most daring work of art of the 21st century they would make it so. They wrote letters to Jonty, insisting he claim the piece as performance, offering to help him frame the event in the appropriate terminology and theories. For all the letters, twenty or more, not one came back till they all came back, every letter sent returned in a large brown envelope. Uta thought it ought to be framed and titled *No Art Enclosed*.

I hear from Gerhard, and he's fixating on David Reed's *Vertigo* piece again. He claims to have recreated the installation from Reed's retrospective at the Kölnischer Kunstverein and to be living inside it. He has spent the last two weeks in bed beneath a copy of painting #328 staring at the TV. He cannot carry on like this; his faculties are dissolving into the otherwise bare walls.

I hear from Gogo who says they can feel their body rotting. Suffocating sex and crap living, too enervated too often to wash much, like most couldn't care anyway: freebie-fucboi can be grimy or whatever, listless semen trap or whatever.

DRESDEN

I DON'T BLAME YOU FOR BEING SO IRREDUCIBLY IMpersonal, I say out loud. I tried it once and it wasn't for me. What hideous eyelids that never shut. But then I tried being smaller, enough to stroke insects – and how cold they must be, I thought. Fucking shocker this being suspended over your isms like so. And I ignore endless spoiler alerts presaging premonitions up ahead. And how is this still a world in which people go out to buy newspapers expecting something to have happened? What the actual nothing. I feel queasy in all these degrees of viscosity. Dystopian democracies under threat of prolapse from all their tiny moving parts. The great horizon behind us, folded up inside a Tetra Pak and it so greasy with remains, of tetrapods no less, our fingers slip. But premonitions are not even the most exciting versions of what we can google the fuck out of. This being so inferior even to ourselves gets so implausibly old, so reborn in bits. Shame humans aren't made of deeper whirlpools, I yawn. The current carries us downstream till the water wakes us and we belch. Some hurled high heels from too much drink. I yawn again. Some kept the rubber tubing in all night. Then the last life spent watching YouTube tutorials for home surgeries. What no mechanisms for enhancing my internal applause? Sad day when even God learns how omnipresence is just some narrative device. Consider the conspiracy of the so-called. Consider me jejunum, duodenum, caecum. Consider me stomached and summarized in a phrase: consider me at your service, at your peril, at a loss for words. I'm writing on your teeth like I had more to say. You know, that surd sound when I pop your abs. That remorseless waste confined to a snort. So goosefleshed, so freshly killed I almost bit my back. The classical harmony of a roadside ditch embossed with everyone anyone is missing. The centrifugal force of our competitive bleeding taking us for ghouls. The swastika'd body hair disappearing behind Geschwind's syndromic brolly. All while a dozen prefabricated confusions (or contusions) in our embedded video presence consider me ripe for live cementing. So do me this one favour before nobody's coming to save me: see to it I'm luminous. See it's a sad day when even our acid's medicinal. See the experimental stenographer scrupulously reversing the sign of the cross is slowly dying from a head cold. I'm all eyes on stalks at everyone's naturalistic dialogue, the supracelestial stereotype of their yuckier perfumes. Goodbye universe in rotation, goodbye remembering the exact amount, goodbye puffy indexical, good luck counting subplots in the torn open voids to remind yourself. Whew silence. Whew the longest proprioceptive sigh. Let me remain falsetto in my lifetime. Let me be. Let's damn the ends. Weep in our downtime.

A world without the distinction between reality and art: Danto warned us. Think of it. Look at it. Every now and then I enter something so real that when

I come out again I'm covered in all these noncircular perversions. And how can a perversion not go round and round? Didn't I always try to hide? Wasn't there always the sense of there being something left that could snap? Where did that go? Our profound dissatisfaction was tinted a mangy, colourless colour, our inadequacies diffuse, our exteriority all recesses, all procedural compensation for the routine comedy of a twitchy indifference – an obliterated literation, a spongy, unreadable, dimensionless piercing of space akin to childbirth some said, as perusable subjects in miniature, religious only about the whereabouts of unvisited surfaces, biological sludge, our curiously translated mouths, the estimated densities of our more spacious neurons to hallucinate this now instead. The prestidigitation of continuous bites and mildewed explosives. The Future's legates come to criminalise all conveyors of free stimulation before it's too late, before there's no money left, an impractical devotion to sound fastening ears to ourselves, rehearsing the intelligence of lard, and me singing on behalf of every uneducable sausage, for every Ling-Ling bereft a body or a head, to give graphorrhea a bad name through just this kind of scribble.

Whatever I end up thinking, Sun Yuan & Peng Yu's *Can't Help Myself* is always running in the background. Kuka industrial robot arm, stainless steel and rubber, cellulose ether in coloured water, lighting grid with Cognex visual-recognition sensors, and polycarbonate wall with aluminium frame all conspire to provide a commentary on the elemental slipperiness of art, for sure, but a nod too (no?) at how frantic and boring it is, this staying alive.

I was reading about them, how they'd diversified, gone off course: Uta, demoralised by her anti-meat activities, embracing heroin addiction instead, or Gerhard breaking into Colditz (reverse engineering the famous British escape of October 14, 1942 by entering the Kommandantur cellar through a dry moat, crossing the courtyard and then climbing up into the POW kitchens and away into the Castle's decaying interior), where he planned to live until discovered; or Gogo, body half-corroded with worse living than they'd anticipated being capable of, taking to drinking the Thames through a long straw as a way of enacting the incumbent impossibilities of any new art.

Gerhard stared into a mirror for as long as he could, until he started being sick, retching uncontrollably when there was nothing left, and collapsed in his chair after 36 hours.

Uta tried to get an artist residence alongside a scientific expedition to Antarctica: a neutrino hunt known as ARIANNA (Antarctic Ross Ice Shelf Antenna Neutrino Array). She thought it would be like *The Thing*, long periods of boredom rewarded with episodes of extreme excitement and metaphysical revelation. When that came to nothing she tried for one at the Large Hadron Collider, thinking maybe she'd get to join *Les Horribles Cernettes*, influence them away from doo-wop into the more fertile soils of contemporary avant-pop.

When I woke from Xavier most of me stayed asleep, no more myself than floating pronouns never coming in to land, going on to root; and yet architecturally and anthropologically – the grand white and grey facades of the buildings opposite rising farther than the sun would allow me to see, the hurried pedestrian glut negotiating my bovine stillness like a stream its surfaced rocks – I ascertained a city, European, French or Spanish or Italian, or perhaps (praise be, could I really have ended up where I was going?) German.

The sounds arrived last and the predominant tongue not Deutsch but Romance, and so many hundreds of miles from Dresden. The time before Xavier coming back then like a pukey-sweet, semi-festered smell. I'd crawled out from the room with a prepacked departure bag left unopened for close to two years. Disappointingly, I knew what it contained without looking – having imagined an immersion more extensive than this, predicted a more arduous period of reacclimatizing to the pre-Xavier entity with whom I was now sharing a body, my failure to foresee how the original motivations of the project could return quite so emphatically stung.

The bag contained money, a passport, maps, routes and addresses. For a second I was Gerhard being Jack Nicholson being David Locke in *The Passenger*, and this wasn't my life at all. And of course it wasn't. Nothing about it was mine that couldn't just as easily have been someone else's. Identity was circumstantial, with not one shred of its evidential trail that couldn't be adopted or manipulated by any number of others at any time.

Whether I was there or not, a few days later I made sure I was somewhere else. It took ten train journeys and twenty-six short taxi rides, going back on myself, in circles a few times, to throw off any tails (we were going to be followed, our leaky plan having seeped into the eyes and ears of certain interested parties whose job it was to prevent the future from happening), to place me outside the agreed hotel in Dresden, stood on the pavement with my one bag looking up into the drizzle and the lights wondering who if any were there already.

Guten tag, or morgen or abend, I forget the precise time the exact greeting before we both continued in English and him giving me the room code, saying how no one else in my group had arrived, and I was expecting three friends, yes? You could call them that, I said, but hopefully friends will be a stretch. He looked at me like his English, though very good, was failing him: equal parts incredulity and embarrassment. Don't worry, private joke, I said, but he didn't smile, seemed sterner than before, as if it was perfectly plausible that the cloistered amusement of a group of strangers was most likely at his expense.

In their absence I'll talk for them: "born of the spirit and born again," I do it for each one, do it over and over. I will dispense with the preliminaries before they arrive. They will pick up the pace soon enough. This needs to be now, as arranged, while the emptiness is nice and crisp.

I look out the window before pulling the curtains to: the street I see and the people walking on it are the type of nondescript I'd hoped for. No one loiters looking up.

Uta provides the opener: what if we created the ugliest thing in the world, and made them love it? Love it so it makes them sick with pain not to be near it. What if they were also repulsed by it? A trypophobe addicted to honeycomb, say. A profound aversion overwhelmed, but only marginally, by an uncontrollable urge, an insatiable appetite for intimacy. Imagine that. Could be fun, no?

We make one for every city in the world, and everything falls apart because nobody can do anything else but…

Reproductions could do the job more effectively, said Gerhard. No need for the proliferation of originals when anyone can have its image on their wall or on their screens. And it needn't be disgusting or beautiful or both – revulsion's overrated. It could be the riddle that consumes them.

The idea is to get everyone, no? An intellectual conundrum won't cut it for the dipshits.

There're all dipshits.

Does it need to be everyone, though? said Gogo, scratching at a raw patch on their forearm. Why not get those smart enough to bite, and leave the rest to fend for themselves? Let the barbarians take over.

A cretinocracy? How would we ever notice?

This can't be it. What would this thing even be? All too theoretical. I had to get them to focus.

What's that you're writing?

This *and* that.

Writing worth anything needs to be perpetrating some kind of crime.

At the very least, against itself.

Like smart phones are destroying your children, what has literature done lately?

One could argue cultural irrelevance is an opportunity for more than wanton obscurity or narrative regurgitation.

If one could take a risk, one would.

Taking a risk implies there's something to lose, when the problem is not the risk itself, or lack of requisite nerve, but identifying exactly what it is might be lost in the process.

Or else there's nothing to lose, and so no such thing as risk.

And so here we are.

I only decided to kill people after reading about all the people I'd killed.

Isn't it still possible to poison the water supply or build a bomb? But not these things, because they don't work.

We need our own tools.

Not more "garbage-tier terrorism." Needs to be bigger.

And smaller.

And subtler.

All of us cooped up in little rooms looking into screens under artificial light with nowhere to go but too far.

And going in circles like we could get there.

THE MUTANT

In the beginning there was Susan. Back when there were five, before the Dresden pact, before we really knew what we were capable of. We gave her the following instructions and she did not deviate. Gerhard filmed her from a distance, hidden cameras in her flat, devoted to her every move till it was over; and not one word exchanged or friendly gesture offered, not one trickle of the humanity we'd vowed to expunge at whatever cost. We kept the performance clean and never showed the footage to anyone. For now there is only what we instructed, there is only this:

You are not the diagnosis. Everyone in the room will want you to be, but it won't happen. The doctor will say the MRI scan was… problematic. She will pause like that. She will be reluctant to use the word *tumour*. Reluctant because cancer spreads, it doesn't roam. And this was moving around inside your head. Appeared independent of the tissues of your brain. But that couldn't be right. They will need to do another scan, but you will refuse. You will know already what you need to know. You will drum your fingers on the desk, and you will say: "In this in-between, chaos becomes rhythm."[1] The remark will be met with consternation. Nobody will talk for at least twenty seconds. As you get up to leave the room, the doctor will also rise from her chair. You will hear her entreating you to come back as you close the door behind you. Having left the building, you can never return.

To be between mutations is to be an even purer possibility.[2] You will feel it. You will feel it like a headache of someone recently decapitated, like the headless part of that equation. Your head is so sweet you can barely swallow it. The facts of the people in that room, the lightbox on the wall, the shining pamphlets, the mannerisms of the auto shop, have degraded in the hours since you left. For your "confectionery head / that draws the cup of fever / is the suicide of truth."[3] What a thing it is, to just be what you are and nothing else; what an accursed state, what a sterile immutability, what a faded god.

You will be living back in your absent mother's cramped flat, in a town you do not consider to be of any particular importance. You know its name and its geographical location but you rarely use it or think of it in those terms. You just feel you are within a margin that borders some other similar but importantly different topography. (But this habit like many others will be subject to change.) Your rooms are the topmost rooms. They are cold in the winter and hot in the summer and most likely insanitary in both. It is a place for walking into things. You know why you live there: "Here in the loft space of the inner edge there is no end for words / they meander through the cluttered strip / these mutant insects violently blinded and driven on / by motors humming in darkness."[4] You know that the hum you hear isn't yet the onset of deafness. You know that the things with which you are colliding aren't yet the result of the pressure in your eyes.

Since leaving the building in which you heard it, in which you thought you heard what you heard but can't be completely sure, because your hearing was perhaps already failing, and what you know you do not know, you have only one enduring notion. You sleepwalk inside it. When the wind is right you can hear Dreamland. You sit on the floor of your room thinking: "I am pursuing only one idea in this dream. What if it were true? What if mutation produced an immortal sub-variety in a given species? What if it existed for any variety? In short, what if we too were immortal?"[5] You will panic as you remember that the idealized condition is never mutable – is always fixed, is always true, is always somewhere else, outside of this inside you've become[6] – and that you embrace mutation at the expense of that.

And they would have you wage war on it. Let their hands climb inside your head and kill it. To make your decision while you can still think, because you cannot think with it. There is no thinking with it, they will say, as if you weren't already. What you know and they don't is that the war can only be an afterthought – the afterthinking of what has already overcome itself, for "war is like the fall or failure of mutation, the only object left for the war machine after it has lost its power to change."[7] You, a mutant, will think alongside this fresh reversioning of your brain. If your speech becomes slurred, you'll see it as a sign of fledgling disembodiment. If you crave your old routines, you'll remember how necrophiles are hooked on those same cravings. You will learn to detach yourself from the world in which this has happened and belong in the itinerancy of not yet having arrived – in the perpetuation of that state.

"Degraded energy has lost its potential to accomplish work, but nevertheless remains in a state of restless mutation."[8] You will have energy only for details. The recursivity of these specifics will consume you. You'll find yourself unable to sleep. The bigger picture will be the smaller picture and vice versa. Nobody will come to visit you where you are going. If you hear a knock at your door, you won't be able to find your way there to answer it. Sitting on your Sierpinski carpet, your head will become a Menger sponge. You will attempt to direct which way to think. Both directions will make you sick. If someone is shouting through your door, the noise will exist somewhere else. You will not be able to decode it and it will not be able to decode you. For a time it will be as if there is no time. You will, in time – in this seemingly timeless time – start to decode the mutations from within. The details will start to destroy you at this point. Your body will quail like brutalized monkeys have been known to do. You will not notice, you will not be there. All there will be "is an abstract machine of mutation, which operates by decoding and deterritorialization. It is what draws the lines of flight: it steers the quantum flows, assures the connection-creation of flows, and emits new quanta."[9]

You will eventually come to, as if arriving back at your-self, as if distances had been travelled that could not have been travelled. You will once again be disorientated to the point of throwing up. You remember someone com-ing "across a series of large charts of mutated chromo-somes," you remember "he rolled them up and took them back to his bunker, [and that] the abstract patterns were meaningless, but during his recovery he amused himself by devising suitable titles for them."[10] You look at what your hands have been doing without you noticing. You see the arrangement of lines repeatedly gouged into your thigh with a pen. You call the auto-written wound some-thing you can only pronounce in your head. The lines do not look like anything that could ever make a sound.

You will dream of plagues. Your eyes will barely function from lack of sleep. You will hear them open and close. Like Saint-Remys you will know that "even destroyed, even annihilated, organically pulverized and consumed to [our] very marrow, […] we do not die in our dreams, that our will operates even in absurdity, even in the ne-gation of possibility, even in the transmutation of the lies from which truth can be remade."[11] As long as you re-fuse to wake up you will not die. You will wonder if you have ever woken up, that even during those times when it seemed as though a bulb of the harshest, nastiest light had been switched on inside your head and would not go out, when you'd seen the outside bathed in that sick glow for months, for years, that perhaps even then you had not really come round. Perhaps even then death had not been near enough to smell you. The women with their faces cut off for fun: perhaps they didn't feel it happen. And the eyes: who's to say they ever saw anything.

You will find eyes distributed about your rooms. An eye will look out from a wall. You will not ever see it blink. You will come to see the eyes as yours. But it won't be through them that you'll see what it is you'll come to see. It will not ingratiate itself to light or the dimensions inseparable from vision. You'll see it without seeing it. Its outline will move and fade and militate against its being one. Anomalous, it will have "no critical incidence in the system. Its figure is rather that of a mutant."[12] If it is to be thought of as tentacled, those tentacles will reach inward – as if to pull itself apart. You will fill a bathtub full of sick from the prolonged unlocatedness of this, from the swell of every durative thought.

"Thus there will come strange jolts, paradoxical mutations, flights that are returns."[13] And you will find yourself back where you started, with torsos shuffling across ceilings and vulvas blooming on withered plants. You will remember the oncologist talking about the finger-like spread of a hypoattenuating peritumoral edema in the white matter that surrounds it. Cracks will appear in walls, in windows, in the floor. Your rooms will fall away beneath you. You will look down at your feet as if down a lift shaft. The world, then, when it returns will do so in bits, in horrific fragments of itself come together in some aleatory nightmare of ever more spasmodic forms. What available light there is will eat your eyes out of their sockets. You will look out from this nowhere of vermicular digestion and vomit your organs into your lap. When your sight returns you will see your vomit is also made of worms, and those worms are made of worms, and so on downward, inward, until you are sick again, and more worms and more sick and so on until your bulimic interiority will speak – and you cannot speak.

"The 'worm' constructs itself out of various previously autonomous systems […] until it coincides – at its most abstract – with a potential for pure contagion. It specializes in nonspecialization, assembling itself out of everything it infects, its nature continuously mutating as it assimilates new material."[14] But then the worm must ask itself: How to infect yourself with everything and once infected turn away from it – to have this aggregation somehow turn away from itself. To live inside this suiciding. To know everything about what it is to know nothing: expert in your own disinterest, in the broad strokes of your ignorance, in the painstaking detail of it. The impossibility of being this meticulously oblivious, this assiduously weary. You will welcome your voided acumen with a kiss. You will that your infinitude become contagious.

Just because it stings at first does not mean it will not carry on stinging. You will panic. You will want to cure yourself. If you could still walk in a straight line, you'd go back to the hospital and beg the surgeons to cut it out, to irradiate it till there's nothing left. But mutation is hard work and it's only right you will lack the necessary resilience at the start. You'll want it to stop, of course. You'll dream of stasis like you were due it. You will again succumb to the weakness of what does not change – to gods, to heavens, to what you are, some tertium quid. You will want to be cured so you can die again, because "it is the cancer cell, in all its protean shape-shifting transformations, that is immortal,"[15] and not this longed-for immutability, this statue up which cats will urinate, and humans climb to afford themselves a better view. Remember, you cannot stay drunk on inertia; you can only live out its fading effects. Your brittleness would feel like dust. Follow your cancer to the end and you will not find it.

Someone is reciting a prayer on the landing outside your door, of which you catch only a fragment: ...Lord have mercy on young girls spreadeagled for horses. Lord have insomnia on account of the world. Lord have mercy on a merciful Lord...

You will experience time. You will experience that same time negate itself: time becoming timeless, becoming other than time. At first you will not know what to do with it. Like you it will be insufficiently diagnosed. In preparing to wait forever you will wait that long. What seem like hours between meals will turn into days. You will ask yourself: "How can time become an acceptance of time, how can it become waiting, patience, and, by a transmutation of patience, eternity?"[16] And something will happen in lieu of all the quotidian happenings repeatedly, laboriously failing to happen. You will think you have found a way to live forever in your dying, in the expanding minutiae of it. But you have a way to go to end up always on the cusp of somewhere else, some further denomination of no-time. There will be a growing hardness in your head, a transfiguring rock, a solidity made soft made hard again. You will vomit its pebbles. The pebbles will crack your sink. The boulder in your skull will strain your neck. The ache around it will mould its contours like putty, penetrate it, form as bubbles of discomfort: an attempted porousness slowly pressurized into precious stones. You will cry diamonds. They will make your tear ducts bleed. You will wet yourself and sit there on the floor in a pool of gem-encrusted fibres. The sarsen in your brain, and of it, will grow and harden and continue to assimilate new forms. You will sense cracks appearing and just as quickly healing. The pressure will become unbearable in that part of you that remains conscious of the duration of such things. Increasingly (which is a word that will be losing its sense by now) "the obelisk ceases to belong to the present and empty world, and it is projected to the ends of time. It rises, immutable – there – dominating time's desperate flight. But even while it is blinded by this domination, madness, which flits about its angles in the manner of an insect fascinated by a lamp, recognizes only endless time escaping in the noise of successive explosions."[17] These explosions will fill your dreams. When the first one happens, tiny fragments of your head will cover the walls and ceiling of the room where you are sitting. A chunk of the exploded rock will break through the floor and smash the skull of the woman who lives below you, whose name you won't recall. She will walk in and out of the rooms of her flat with a piece of still-palpating stone protruding from her head. She will sing the songs she used to sing to her grandchildren before they moved away. She will not expire from her injury as quickly as you expect. The nursery rhyme becoming increasingly mangled will turn into something else. Interspersed with the faltering rhyme you will hear her sing the words: "Mutants are cowards."[18] The woman will appear to gloat as she looks up through the hole in her ceiling at those fragments of you stuck to your own ceiling. You will be all over your room at once. The constrained force will vanish with the disintegration of your head. When all the pieces finally retract to their original positions before the explosion, the pressure will return. You will wait for subsequent explosions to arrive. The threat will taste to you like metal. You will vomit an arched projectile made of glass.

(…Say something then! What's up, cancer got your tongue?)

Dwelling on the words – "mutants are cowards" – you will begin to feel like one. You will for a few seconds want someone near you, so you won't have to be near yourself. You talk out loud as if someone hearing it might take the words away with them. That they might never come back. That you could eventually use every combination and there'd be no materials left with which to think. You feel the hard lump pushing against the inside of your right ear. You think you bite the back of your tongue. It bleeds sentences you cannot form and cannot endure. You feel your brain turn to concrete.

The sound of rain will sound like so many other things you will not be able to keep track, but it is just the sound of rain. Not fragments of a disintegrated space station, having somehow evaded the atmosphere. Not the suicidal lunacy of tiny birds. Not the echo chamber of your skull echoing. It is not the sound of your brain popping epiphanies like zits, or finessing its folds in search of an owner.

In the early mornings, before the old woman below you (is her name Elsa?) starts shouting at her cat, and the man in his early twenties (whose name you know is Sivart from the visitors he has, who shout up from the street to let them in, but then perhaps it is Travis, because you've heard that too), across the hall has reached over from his bed to turn his music on (Trap or UK Drill all day, most of the night), you will hear the sea breaking against the harbour walls. You will imagine the Turner Contemporary wreathed in spray. You imagine its hard white facades turned porous like a sponge, its edges coming apart, its entire geometry softened as if into the finest shingle by the relentless crashing of the sea. Without looking you will see the grey foam collecting in the corners of the gallery steps, in the gutters in the road. You see Sivart in his bed, his skunky brain crawling across his face and it's every bit as mutated as yours. And though you do not see any legs it's still as if it crawls, as if there are a thousand or more tiny legs protruding from its underside, conveying its folded mass, the sulci the gyri rising and falling as if the skin of some grotesque mammal labouring for breath, over the sunken musculature of his face and down his extended arm. You return then to the permeable outline of the decimated waves and the Turner Contemporary, the amorphous fuzz of it: *"a line that delimits nothing, that describes no contour*, that no longer goes from one point to another but instead passes between points, that is always declining from the horizontal and the vertical and deviating from the diagonal, that is constantly changing direction, a mutant line of this kind that is without outside or inside, form or background, beginning or end and that is as alive as a continuous variation – such a line is truly an abstract line, and describes a smooth space."[19] You return again without looking, because you've seen it already, down and to the left, through the chip trays careering into lampposts and cars like drugged birds, through the clouded double glazing filling with rain, your eyes as though sand is in them blurring and sore.

There won't be any more returns to King's Cross, to that building on Granary Square. Your train pass will have expired one week when you come across it on the floor beside the bed. Your post-grad work will become this: your brain mutations in your mother's three small rooms, while she is pissed somewhere with the man she met who doesn't like children, especially ones past thirty, who never means to do any of the things he does, who could punch holes in faces he doesn't like and does and who punches holes much lower down in those he loves, so as not to be reminded of them, and who lives far enough down the coast for you to never have to rehearse what you might say should they ever come back. You will eat from the tins she left in preparation for throwing up. The food therein will in texture and taste resemble the purge it begets.

Picture the organs of revenants. Picture what they'd look like, what functions they might perform. Picture any one of those revenant's organs suspended in mid-air, arranged diagrammatically as if there was still some human form maintaining their composition. Picture this picture's gradual reconfiguration, the organs drifting free from their natural neighbours, taking up residence in other people's hands, in empty windows, in the defoliated limbs of trees.

You will remember being inside the Turner Contemporary standing over a drowned body. You will remember a man's hair growing at a ridiculous speed. You will remember the names: you remember Jeremy Millar, you remember Tehching Hsieh. Their names seem to refer not to the artists but to infinitesimally small parts of the cancer. Are you calling it that now? It's possible you might come to use it as shorthand. You might come to regard the rest of your body, the area outside your head, as its metastasized form – as the congealed progeny of your brain growth, with its own traits and foibles and means of conducting itself, as the mutation of a mutation. You're somehow foreign to it, waiting for it to die, to die without you. Knowing it's "mutation makes the fetus abort. And [how] with that, the parasite – the assassin – commits suicide."[20] You will see baby rats spinning webs in the corner of the room like they did in Philip K. Dick's "Recall Mechanism." You remember the Precogs were so named because they could see the future, and that they were mutants too. These vatic statements are not instructions. You look out your window and see a seagull eating vomit from a bench.

Invoking Raymond Roussel's confession (that one the day before he suicided), a thought happens somewhere in French: *j'ai* écrit *une partie de ceci*. You write it down in English: *I wrote some of this*. You are going mad in another language altogether. Roussel died from a barbiturate overdose. He had run out of money that you never had. You hear from an unsubstantiated source how he was astonished to be dead. You are going mad in a language that no one gets to read – because no one ever wrote in it. You are going mad with the thingness of words. You've watched them become self-conscious to the exclusion of being conscious of anything else. You watch them play; you watch them eating each other. They move like insects over a forest floor. You make out what they allow you to make out. They are making you up. You make out "mutant abstract lines that have detached themselves from the task of representing a world, precisely because they assemble a new type of reality,"[21] and the forest becomes a sea of sawdust, and an old woman screams for her cat, lying stiff on the roadside covered in ants, caught in the web the rats have made, body cocooned in silk, meowing prayers to the one God, and Travis's music that sounds like a headache inside that God. And you outside of Him, where "there is nothing but – nothing" for "it is impossible that anything of change or mutability can get into God."[22] You will meow like a cat that's talking to God. You will change into a disguise that disguises your changing.

A floating proboscis in a floating vein. Weightless seeing levitating over a soiled bed, its urine-yellow pillows,
its frayed and blood-stained fitted sheet, what is left of
you "like an eye popping out of its socket, hanging on
the end of its optic nerve, scanning the horizon through
180 degrees but not sending back any images – a disembodied panoptical terminal, runaway organ of a species
of mutants."[23]

On the surface not a uniform grey, but the grey of some
underlying fundament always leaching through, the entire town, the whole coastline like a once brightly painted
lead now weathered faint and cracked and peeling. The
beaches and promenade deserted but for dog walkers,
and immiserated, weary-looking drunks failing to nego-
tiate straight lines, and equally weary-looking teenagers
in pissy shelters grinding the last of their bud and bitch-
ing at the interminable blackness of the sea like it could
hear, like it could care, like that same blackness wasn't
also behind them.

The mini-series of your body is stuck on repeat. The way
the perverts bite into children's legs, that's as raunchy as
your afternoon can get. And anyway, the death you're diagnosed with won't happen. Those deaths never happen.
A prognosis doesn't know how to kill.

Sivart is watching *The Transfiguration* for the 92nd time.
It's the part where Milo is watching himself through a
closed door: soldier-straight, side on, coat zipped up all
the way, black bin bag in his left hand. (His mother's
room, her suicided in there, the blood he'll drink, his

madeleine moment, his Humbert Humbert moment, his
footnote for the habit he's acquired.) He has his hands
down the front of his tracksuit bottoms. Smoke churns
from the ashtray. He can't hear what Milo's brother and
Milo are saying for the music, but he mouths the words:
What the fuck you doing? Nothing. At the foot of his bed
a book on Dennis Nilsen is lying open. Two sketches:
Wardrobe Melrose Avenue, a dead body crumpled in the
lower left-hand side, on the right-hand page the body on
the floor, tie round its neck, socks still on, posed as if
running, ritual stripping and washing the body, a pair
of trousers standing on their own, roughly circular stain
in the crotch. That guy was a faggot, right? The shape,
thirteen-or-so, in the corner chair, nose fuming like a
dragon. Lonely is lonely, says Travis, taking his hand out
the front of his trousers. Flushed his lovers down the lav,
right? "These things have all the incoherence of dreams
without the alibi of sleeping. They hover like bats over
the soul's passivity, or like vampires that suck the blood
of submission."[24] What the fuck is that? Another shape,
late teens, sat on the floor, thin, hunched over: He mem-
orizes quotes about vampires.

Your skin is pale and squirming: maggots in cheese. You
will come across your thoughts like they happened in
someone else's head. You will squint in the sunlight like
everybody else. The outside feels cold going in. You're
decaying at room temperature. That thought you had of
being alive next year leaves a nasty-looking blister.

Who's the old cunt buries birds in the back garden?
Your mother on the phone, bored, shitfaced, remembering you exist for the time it takes to make the call.
You answering all agitated, mistaking it for something
else, pawing at it, hearing the voice as if from that imagined grabbed-at thing. He died. You know him, ground
floor, old suit, greasy hair. Yeah, he died. Yeah, but you
remember him. Manifestly, so what? What was his
name? No idea. She don't know, told yah she wouldn't,
no bother, love. Was that it? You well, love? Apart from
the brain cancer, you mean? You what? Yeah, I'm fine.
Good. You know we're too obvious to exist, right? Of
course, yeah; I'll call again soon.

Your condition will progress from crisis to catastrophe.
That you have headaches without a head won't matter.
That you have many more than one headache at once will
be resolved. That your head is missing while also larger
and heavier than the largest, heaviest rock on Margate
beach, on Dover beach, on any of the south coast's various outsized litter trays, their "eternal note of sadness,"
their "eternal ebb and flow of human misery"[25] intact,
will be of no concern, will be relegated to some ancient
history of the real. Your thoughts reaching your mouth
to be realized as belches, as little trickles of acrid sick
rising in the open-topped throat, "the irruption of something anomalic, which functions according to rules and
forms we do not and may never understand."[26]

Nobody sees you at the bottom of the pond. Nobody
sees you breathing. What is it you're breathing down

there? Is it the insects after they've drowned? Look at them staring all wrong: they can't even see the horse's head inside your head.

You will write things down in an effort to systematize what is going on. The system will break down before you are finished, before you've really got started. You will give one of them a title (Cartesian Mutationism) that will inadequately surmise what you are thinking. It will begin with 3 core theses:

T1) I (as a corruption/a wound of substance) am an obliteration, a non-extended thinking mass

T2) My body is the scab that seeks to heal the breach (the festering non-entity) of invisible unclaimed I-gaps

T3) I am really a hole/a hollow excavated from my body and so can exist (as holes exist as pockets of emptied space) without it

On the grounds that it was only after establishing the existence of God that Descartes was able to establish the existence of his own body, you will argue that that "I" always presents itself violently to the body, and that the body acts as a nullifying balm to the "I", corroborating the flesh regardless of God's omnipotence and immanent sincerity. You will go on to say how this nothing is itself qualified: it is a nothing of a something, an excavation, a clawed-out space, and so to propose separation would be to remove the hole from that in which it exists as a hole.

Descartes thought he could pretend that the hollow has no borders in the soil of the body, that it is essentially extraneous to any world he could conjure, but he could not, or so he thought, pretend that this gap-made-substance didn't exist. He concluded that he was this manifest absence, and that its essence was to think, a process requiring no place or material instantiation – a non-thing entirely distinct and independent of physicality.

Your nails will grow all the better to gouge your eyes out with. And what's underneath them doesn't even qualify as dirt, for what brand of dirt is it that has quite that many fully functioning legs?

You will write like you are getting somewhere, but you are not. You will make unsubstantiated claims. You will write: The self is an excavated void, the empty core of the unified origin of thought. Again: A hole is not a nothing, but a nothing in a something: an excavation. The authentic is the hole, but you can't live there. You will tie yourself up in convoluted speculations: The doubter of the corporeal is a disembodied substance – turned on itself it should perceive only incorporeality. The self hunts itself back to nothing – the empty something at the heart of constitution. Emptiness is a nothing that suggests a something, and that something is shape. I am intelligible as a nothing instantiated by somethings, a nothing whose particularity of placed-vacuity can be understood as non-essential. This understanding implies that the excavated void of self can in principle be separated from the thing in which it was hewn, is distinct and so can exist without it. The something of the body and the brain is divisible, but a void is not. You cannot dissect what isn't there.

You will shit from your mouth and vomit from your anus. You will attract no new lovers. Your uterus will ulcerate and bleed. Your vulva will decompose. You will cuckoo your brain into a womb. Bedbugs nourish you in your sleep. The light Turner saw outside your window glows in your intestines. The meaning of the sky and the sea is pain, is lather: a washbasin of chopped-up rabbits and suds.

Your handwriting will become more erratic, almost illegible in places: My thoughts are attributed to a void, an apparition of empty agency, so it is (I am) essentially the nothing that thinks. I am a nothing in a something, a nothing that moves and is moved. This story is explanation enough – a simple account of what happens, of the interactions (temporary interminglings) between a nothing and a something – that are both nothings, both somethings. How is it that the nothing can have causal influence in the material world? The truth of ghosts and selves is (Ducasse's) Proximate Causation. It's built into the myth, a brute fact of that myth, and the myth mirrors and is mirrored in the world. All regularities are tales of mystery and suspense. The excavation and the excavated cause each other.

The last words of this dyspeptic screed are smudged across the page like you had cried on them, or spat, or drooled: Self-consciousness: The echo of the shape that postulates a hole. The groping at the nothing to find the shape of its nonexistence. The futility of echolocation in a black hole. Introspection: the excavation process offered up to the cavity it creates.

You will hear the fucking gulls. You will hear the fucking gulls screaming that the sea is still there, that hunger is still there existing without you, that you are not the only one that can hover in the air above your bed.

But still you will not have given up on space, on building something in it/of it – of transforming that ephemeral canker into a living space for some different sort of living. You will have notions that space can be remade from its inaccurate replication. You contemplate climbing into the cupboards in the kitchenette and like some excommunicated child erecting elaborate collapsing architectures from the lack of room in there, and have them stand "as something like an imperative to grow new organs to expand [y]our sensoria and [y]our bodies to some new, as yet unimaginable, perhaps ultimately impossible, dimensions."[27] Perhaps you will actually do this – it might be up to you; and, ignoring the spiders you find, the rats in their webs gnawing through their runted litters, you might proliferate experimental organs the functions of which you cannot know. You might come to see these organs fill the cupboard space, spill out to fill the kitchenette, spill farther still to annex the bedroom, the toilet, rupturing windows and doors, consuming the whole building. You will see space not so much occupied as excoriated. Sivart will smile with crenelated teeth. His gestures will materialize outside of him, in the objects in his room, in the organs silently growing inside those objects. Every liminal structure constructed out of your confinement will delimit the area within which death might expedite itself. You think about putting your head in the oven, but the oven is electric and your head is too swollen with organs to fit. You will see yourself where you are not. Some of the new organs will wear a face that resembles your own so as to be just so many iterations of it. All these mutative extravagancies are in essence a returning, in which every particle in the universe "must see its own identity swallowed up in difference, each being no more than a difference between differences."[28] Every drop of seawater flooding the steps of the Turner Contemporary was something else before it was a wave, a puddle, a thing you saw engulf a gallery like an apparition destitute of form.

You will cut your nipples off in a panic. Imagine feeding something else with the excreta you could make. You will drink some water and it will thicken in your throat. The pigeons on the roof will kill each other to distract you from their imperfections. The blood will look like it came from any kind of bird. Your consciousness will scab over. You are the daughter of an over-lacquered hairdo. You are the daughter of a sunspot, a body of wet sand, a wedding figurine bent like a user's spoon. You will sleep like the deer that barely sleep at all.

Because "all the images of paradise, of glorious souls and bodies, or the commonplace representations of the dead reincarnated by metempsychosis, have never kept the true, immutable domain of death from remaining that of a chilling fear,"[29] you will fabulate using only already spoiled materials.

You will discover infinite substrata in a sea of nerve-endings. You will bleed into your trousers one morning and it will hurt. You will bang on the floor when the old woman is wailing for the police to resurrect her cat. You will hardly notice Sivart's music anymore; but when the voices in there are raised or they erupt into hysterics, the bloated congeries of your own thoughts will no longer be able to ameliorate the intrusion. When Travis is out you will hear the old woman's TV, left on full volume so it can follow her as she shuffles from room to room in search of one or other of some half-dozen missing cats. This acousmatic arrangement is something you share.

The mornings will not recognize themselves. They will be there in spite of you. The times of the day will evince only the baseless corruptions of something, exquisite and terrifying, that cannot be divided. There will be no more dereliction of purpose, only a single purpose of dereliction. It will not be the content of your experience but your complete immersion in its happening, and your relative inexperience in imagining any cogent outside to this uncertain somewhere, that will desensitize you to your body and its waning functions. You will suffer happiness like you once suffered pain; you will suffer pains like they are the agonies of someone you love. You will start to recognize yourself in the objects around you. The seagulls have messages and you must listen to what they say. Travis's noise is a code you must decipher. Passers-by on the street are shills embroiled in the unique collusions of your dying. In other words, in the words of some other, "the brain mutation that is underway can be described as a spasmodic attempt to cope with the surrounding chaotic infosphere and to reframe the relation between infosphere and the brain. [...] The adaptation of the brain to the new environment involves enormous suffering, a tempest of violence and madness."[30] The violence is unavoidable. And it is yet to arrive. Do not shirk its implications in the hope of assuaging some greater threat. There is no getting outside and staying outside. And the glimpses from there, from that extra-frangible cocoon of not being mad, only prolong the ordeal of some exhaustive and codified notion of human sanity.

The impairment to your hearing will come and go. If you can hear me, it's your own voice that's coming through. Remember to inseminate every new instant with the next. Remember the crushing sound in your head is just your head being crushed.

You will imagine returning to the hospital, to the oncology ward, your legs giving out from under you in the waiting room, looking up at all the "wan-faced pseudo mutants with eyes like blind fish"[31] tepidly waiting for their treatments. However scared you get you will not suffer the indignity of that. "Mutants built their own shelters out of saliva and ash;"[32] they do not need their gamma knives and radiotherapy, their shunts and their chemo, their considered prognoses and statistical variance. Mutation like life is dangerous. Mutation is the noise of the message conveying its own message. There is no such thing as a managed end, only an end to management, a wilful relinquishment of control. "Stop sending your ships through the narrow cosmo-logical corridor. Stop making them climb the extreme walls of the world. *Let* them jump over the cosmic barrier and enter into the hyperspace of the Universe. Cease having them compete with light, for your rockets too can realize the more-than-psychic, postural mutation, and shift from light to black universe which is no longer a colour; from cosmic colour to postural and subjective black. Let your rockets become subject of the Universe and be present at every point of the Remote."[33] The ziplock bag in the kitchen cupboard with your ovaries inside: you can eat them whenever you like.

Your skin will turn the grey of Margate beach. The grey of the forgotten economy-meat-eating patrons of its greasy spoons. The grey of faded newspaper print and burnt-down cigarettes and 60s Brutalist high-rise flats. The grey of the diseased matter in your head. The grey of the dream you have of somewhere else. And as for the colours that aren't grey – because for all its symbolic felicity no seaside town is shaded so homogenously – they are the greyest versions of themselves, and could not be greyer without thereby ceasing to be examples of variance, however nugatory. Just to smell you is to sense the spiders getting fat.

Your intestines will congeal like cooked spaghetti, like flies over a lake. And between the planets of the gallery and your rooms there are your legs stuttering like they may never get started. You're overthinking the simplicity of what they can do. You've attributed them a different life from your own, and the weight of it crushing them. When your legs slide from the bed there'll be no story to help you compute how it was done.

What happens next is dictated by the process. It cannot be documented in advance, and any stipulations around it must remain tentative at best, as "the initial escape from form is represented by a process of unpredictable mutation." You see snakes caught in webs the rats have made. You see them in the intestines of a suspended horse. The severed heads in a row in front of you wear the same expression. All the disembodied organs are similarly fetal. Every fragment dismembers; every dismemberment fragments. Then it's all a blur. There are fleeting resemblances. You're choking: there's a cock in your mouth facing the wrong way. You're surrounded by desert. Its contours are reflected in the sky. The vision is particulate and strained and discharged of belonging. There are areas of blackness scratched at to establish flimsy increments of light. "Beyond the mutant there is a superior amorphousness, belonging to the monster that has no intrinsic form of its own, or even an inherent morphological trajectory."[34]

The six-legged men will gather among the trees and masturbate each other with their broken teeth. The world is ending tomorrow and the drunks are drunk. Old women are groping at a child. Ice cream is melting down its arm. At the edge of what you can see: translucent worms eating eyeballs out of heads. The world is ending tomorrow and the horror of boredom. A woman no longer has the bulk to keep her trousers up; she lets them drop only so far; she plays the fistula in her arm like a penny whistle. Hurry, the sea is turning black! Hurry, the memory is in my throat!

You will get the urge to walk and you will submit to it. You will leave your rooms, descend the stairs and go out into the street. You will turn to the left and walk in that general direction until…: She dead or what? Fucking state of her. She needs an ambulance. Wait, she's coming round. You alright, love? Shall we call someone? Is that blood? What did she say? I can't hear her; shut up a minute! What did she say? "Processes of mutation are in general highly volatile. During the mutation, the relationship between the organism and its environment is perturbed, redefined as stochastic, fragile, probabilistic."[35] The fuck's that supposed to mean? Must've hit her head going down. What's she smiling about? You will stand up and walk away from the people gathered there. You will not look back or explain yourself. Silently traduced in turn by everyone you pass, the invigoration will begin: the kind of abject necessity you might see in a dog eating its own shit. Without planning to you will head in the direction of the beach.

Someone has followed you. He is overweight with greying hair and a reddened face. The skin around his eyes is folded

and sallow. You need to eat something. Come! Come! He
takes your arm and guides you into a chip shop. He leans
you up against the counter and makes your order. Is she
okay? She just needs some food; we found her on the floor.
The man behind the counter is tall and Turkish and cannot stop looking at you. When he slides the tray of chips in
front of you, you will lift your head. Smiling, he says: "The
'xeno-agent' or radical outsider never appears as a discrete
entity or individuated substance beyond vague indications
of motion and fog, but is revealed only nebulously on the
ground (the superficial or visible outside) through symptoms of transmutation and madness."[36] You turn to the
other man, who is nodding and grinning. He's right, you
know: eat those up and then get yourself to the hospital.
He goes for his wallet, but the other man holds his hand
up and shakes his head. Thanks. He touches you on the
arm – you'll be alright – and waves and leaves. On a bench
outside you will stare at the chips. Seagulls will be there,
waiting. You will lift up a chip and put it down again.
When you eventually eat one it is nearly cold. You feel it
going down. You feel it coming straight back up. You eat
another and another. You eat them all as if the aggregate
weight will keep them from coming back up. Less than a
minute later the retching will sound to you like a new kind
of speech pattern, a "mutation of language into style under
the impulse of an unnameable otherness, which, passional
to begin with, then acquires rhythm before becoming
empty." You will see the barely masticated rectangles as
if they were a jumble of words – no sense, no meaning.
You come to realize that you are "comfortable only in the
presence of *the nothing-at-all, the void*,"[37] and that you do

not inhabit your stomach, that comfort is no place for the living, and that by dying you are becoming increasingly alive, fiercely so, agonizingly foreign to your death.

You will throw up until you are virtually inside out. When you throw up your brain you'll feel compelled immediately to eat it. It will smell just like the brain you are missing. The way it retains its shape and size, it's almost as if it's been eaten before, almost as if it was born there in your head regurgitated and had never been anywhere else.

You're sure people can see the light streaming out of your head, forcing its way through the cracks and fissures, the whitest, cleanest light, the freeze-framed explosion of a star. You're sure it's blinding them so that you can see everything. Nothing is hidden. The number of lumens, if you could count them, would be consonant with your skeletonizing the universe, the candela-count in the centre of your brain in the many billions and rising. No secrets left just light, just everything exposed, just the rupturing harmony of your human powerlessness evis-cerated for some idea of some perfect eye. "A mutation takes place in the history of secrecy. If the light was in the world, if it had its source outside and not within us, within the spirit, one would be able to conceal objects, cities, nuclear arms. The object wouldn't disappear but be hidden behind a screen. [...] But once the light is in us, within the interiority of the spirit, then secrecy is no longer possible."[38]

The man in the dark grey suit on The New King's Stairs has already raped and eaten the girls he is watching.

He is enjoying their reconstituted amusement. However many times he tears them into little pieces they manage to reassemble themselves to play at being little girls again. But he can see the joins and you can see him seeing the joins. When you claw at his face, his indignation is whatever innocence looks like on the outside. He is mimicking the faces of the heads he's cut off. You tell him that, and he looks around him at the assembling bystanders and begs an explanation for what you're saying. She's not right in the head. I don't know what she's talking about. But he does and you keep talking, and your hands are round his neck.

You will catch reflections of some gaunt thing looking back at you. When they smile they are horror-movie smiles. All mouths bent up like that share this same unnerving origin. Like the teeth are bulletproof, like the sentiment's malicious for being grounded in nothing. The opulence of their boredom is strangers politely spitting in your face.

Inside you death is suiciding. A disease becomes diseased, and that diseasing of the disease diseased in turn. Your exterior is a vulnerability you no longer recognize. "It is at this mobile and precise point, where all events gather together in one that transmutation happens: this is the point at which death turns against death; where dying is the negation of death, and the impersonality of dying no longer indicates only the moment when [you] disappear outside of [your]self, but rather the moment when death loses itself in itself, and also the figure which the most singular life takes on in order to substitute it-self for [you]."[39]

In your dream, they are soldering your genitals onto the side of a bus. Outside it, your face is flaking off on your mother's pillow. Somewhere in between, light is coming through the window in bloodstained gloves.

When everything else is on show, whatever was left of you will be gone. Not hidden but evaporated. Not de-stroyed but absorbed. "The great disappearance is not, then, simply that of the virtual transmutation of things, of the mise en abyme of reality, but that of the division of the subject to infinity, of a serial pulverization of con-sciousness into all the interstices of reality."[40] When Siv-art and his friends come across you sitting on the stairs leading up to your landing – when they comment on the blood-stained tracksuit bottoms, the matted hair, the patches shaved back to the skin, the bare feet turning black, the words coming out of your mouth that come from nowhere and go nowhere – you are everywhere else becoming invisible. It's your invisibility that they're taken with. If you were there they'd tire of your presence on the stairs long before they do. They wouldn't touch you like that. They wouldn't spit. (How can they say it is your breath that stinks so incontrovertibly of shit? How can they say it was you waiting for them and not them for you?) The old woman wouldn't inquire about the where-abouts of her cat before calmly descending the stairs. The things that go inside you would remain outside. The couple from the ground floor, taking a break from their reciprocated disgust, would do more than shout upward to quell the noise. (How loud you might have whimpered had you hung around to find out.) If you were there, what is happening would be happening to you. But as it is you've disappeared. In all the cracks in which you're invisible, the world is happening somewhere else.

This is a maculate conception: the legs of a brain unpicked and prised apart, that slim and pretty virgin out of *Sodom* deflowered with a turd.

What the canker thinks will not get spoken. There aren't the words for where it's going, for what it is, for what you are in its being otherwise and anonymous; so that when you hear it, when you hear yourself, as if you exist in some one place and time and can be said to have spoken, the language will bear the mark only of a chronic instability, a mutability of meaning, a volatile spew of half-remembered noises approximating what was only ever half-said and heard as something else. Like this "a mutation occurs […] and the absolute heterogeneity of these two spaces (the translated and the translating), leaves the mark of a transmutation on the body of the translation."[41] What they see, the mess of you: that's the measure of this bad translation. That slab of convulsing granite inside your head, an open wound with no outside, is what it means to poorly paraphrase the form of some formless thing, its voice the voice of a swamp, its syntax the syntax of something travelled there to drown. You will see the language of this swamp as some broadly viral component and those attempts to have it understood as speculative serums, but nothing ever comes back: "A virus mutates its code faster than vaccines can be developed for it; a game of cloak-and-dagger ensues, and the virus vanishes by the time it is sequenced, having already mutated into another virus."[42]

The couple downstairs are pissed. Their baby is screaming. It's 9.30 in the morning. The small garden behind them is full of dead birds. He is useless. She is useless. The baby is fucking crying. Travis is asleep with both his TVs on. The old woman is sitting on her sofa watching *J'ai Pas Sommeil* again. She looks over at her front door every few minutes, and repeatedly gets up and goes to check the locks. She peers out through the peephole, gently hopping up and down to relieve the pain in her bad hip. You are floating above your bed bleeding from the ears. A seagull is pecking at your window. You remember your mother used to throw her scraps on the roof. "What separates [you] from the immensity, those differentiated contents that memory represents to [you], does not signify that [you are] a given object in the order of objects that God rules over, but that, in the immutable immensity, equal to itself, what [you are] is at *issue*."[43] You make clicking sounds with your mouth. Your body is twitching: tiny convulsions, so many mice under your skin dying on their backs. Your brain is on the other side of the room trying to eat from a tin of baked beans. Its surface is blistered and tentacled with thin wormlike protrusions. You look over at the bed and no one is there. You hear the seagull scratching at the roof.

The way everything continues is not comforting. The way your teeth dissolve, like sugar in hot water, doesn't even come close. Sweating that way, the way you are sweating now, your skin so many faucets the room an equatorial forest, should not be mistaken for a purge. Nothing will cleanse anything else. The snare inside you will not open.

The sun will create a shaft of warmth and light through the room. When you place your hands in it you will be able to feel them again. Your head inside it will be freed of the weight of its being there. You will fill the room like smoke. It's your face on Sivart's two screens. You are telling him he needs to wake up. You are the plumes rising from his ashtray. You are the faint clouds of water vapour coming out the mouth of the old woman. She is stroking her lap as if there's a cat. You will tell Travis that it's okay for him to masturbate over those Nilsen drawings in his book. You will order him to do it while you watch. You will talk him through it, you will seduce him. When he's finished you will both be sick in your mouths and swallow it. Curling up into a ball you will hug your own cadaver. Your eyes will float in a pool of someone else's blood. You are every individual part of the smoke now trailing down the hallway, down the stairs. You will be breathed in by the baby on the ground floor so that its head will explode when the father throws it at the wall.

You repeat to yourself how it is that "without a profound complicity with natural forces such as violent death, gushing blood, sudden catastrophes and the horrible cries of pain that accompany them, terrifying ruptures of what

had seemed to be immutable, the fall into stinking filth of
what had been elevated – without a sadistic understanding of an incontestably thundering and torrential nature,
there could be no revolutionaries, there could only be a revolting utopian sentimentality."[44] And yet you cannot help
feeling that in spite of your mutability you are ascending,
and that this suffering is flagrantly unnatural – that these
accumulating horrors are some bleed-through from some
other world, and syrupy too, and idyllic, for what do they
stand for but a superstructure that somehow censures this
behaviour from afar. Horrors shored up by the dream that
they might not happen.

You will go to see the souls at the zoo. To see them biting
at each other, fighting over food. You will turn on the TV
expecting to see them there. The zoo is a supermarket, a
crowded beach. Everybody squanders themselves in the
dark. Someone is poisoning the humans, and they like
it. Someone is growing a ghost to haunt the living they
have left. You are preparing to haunt no one in particular, and by that logic everyone. The dead are only dead if
someone remembers them. You remember the pills they
prescribed – for as long as it takes to forget them. You
grieve in advance. You grieve in a dress, with rips in the
hem, without butterflies. You grieve like grass. You can
smell it happening. You smell blood in the sugar bowls in
the cafe you wake up in.

You ("the postmodern urban individual mutant") will be
"required to become not even a thing, but simply a [mist
of] blind, furious particle[s]."[45] You will be required to

embody this disembodiment, to become your unbecoming, to fuse with your diaspora. The permutations of your mutation will be endless – there will be no commutation of this mutation, only further transmutations, only mutation after mutation after mutation. You will descend into delirium, into head pain, into seagulls and noise and waves of sick and every speck in every eye of those watching as you come apart.

It feels like the jet lag you'd have if you'd been flying your entire adult life, setting off in a time-zone without time, to arrive here on Earth.

No longer complicit in "the cancerous metastasis of [the individual's] basic formula,"[46] you will metastasize a new formula, an anti-formula, the individual as swamp, as fog, as haze, as the infinite perforations in a lump of air.

Having dragged yourself up the front steps of the Turner Contemporary, leaning heavily on the railings to keep yourself upright, your limbs on the steps turning momentarily to slush, you will continue in the same direction until you are inside the building. You will head straight for the gallery space on the ground floor. You will already have attracted the attention of at least two members of the gallery staff with your staggering, with your bumping into things, with your smell. You are littering the floor with copies of this artist's statement. You are wearing filthy clothes. You are mumbling. Your legs do not appear to be under your full control. You can barely walk. You will arrive at a point equidistant from the walls and stop. Turning your back to the huge windows, to the north light, to the sea, you will announce yourself. The performance will begin. A heavy outflux of fluid will run down your legs and pool at your feet. One of your eyes will fall out. The sides of your skull will bulge and distort and squeal. Your head will swell to twice its original size. It will fracture and leak. Someone will throw up that isn't you. The people in there will multiply. They will be jostling to get a better view. The gallery staff, the two security guards, will want to intervene, but nobody is sure if the event is sanctioned, and they are nervous with the ambiguity. This and what is happening to your body keeps them away. They talk on phones as if they are selling you at auction. You are filmed at every angle by the crowd. There will be no sense of how conspicuous you are, how exposed and scrutinized. Your head will continue gathering strange accretions. The entire process becomes iterative: you, the discomfort of the onlookers, the sea outside marking the same bleak rhythm. The whole gallery poised, the air thinner somehow, the light disfiguring, the sounds of breathing a lullaby, your thoughts hardening, xenolithic. The sense then that you are falling and there is no end to it.

What is that? What's happening to her neck? (Your body is still upright, but you are falling.) Oh shit. Is this fucking happening? What's that snapping noise? Ugh, sounds like… (Your ribs are breaking.) She's pregnant. She's pregnant. Is someone going to help her? Her stomach shouldn't be that big. (You were pregnant; you are pregnant again.) Someone has to do something. Why is nobody doing anything? Look, there, see it? Oh my God.

What the fuck. Where? I can't see, what? Between her legs. There's something between her legs. Is that a fucking tentacle? No, no, no, no... I feel sick. Fuck, what was that? (Your pelvis has shattered.) She's bleeding. That's so much blood. Oh my God, it's everywhere. Her tracksuit bottoms... they can't stay up. Oh fuck! Shit! Fucking hell. Oh no, no, no, no... It's her fucking brain; it's her fucking brain; it's her fucking brain... Shut up! Shut up! Shut up!... The head. The head, look. It's collapsing. (Your head is falling apart.) There's nothing inside. It's empty. It's empty. The baby is moving. The brain is crawling. The baby's alive. It's stopped. It's dying. The brain is dying. The baby is dying. Someone do something!

They will not scrape your remains up off the floor as a means of disposal, but will instead slide a thin sheet of clear Perspex underneath it as a way of preserving what you've become. It will catch on your flayed skull and they will need to coax it up with a metal spatula. They will add five more square sections of thicker Perspex (also clear) to form a cube around you. They will slide another sheet of Perspex, the same thickness as the other five, underneath the thin base sheet. They will title it: "The Mutant." After they seal the edges, the air inside will be replaced with formaldehyde.

Only, the last part didn't go as planned. It wasn't up to her, the remains scooped up and housed in Perspex like that. Instead, the gallery staff cleared the room, the police arrived, declared it suicide, made out how she was mentally ill, the phone footage shared online dismissed as a hoax. They buried the remains. She went away. People forgot. Not those present for the show, but eventually their voices waned, their protestations fizzling out till no one much thought about it anymore. Our fifth member all but squandered, and yet we learned the price of what it means to be alien, to be unconcerned by the petty vacillations of human identity and emotion. The price is this subsequent hush, this fortification of follies, this never-ending perpetuation of the same. We learned it wasn't enough to show – they could see anything and carry on – we needed to transform.

NOTES

1. See Gilles Deleuze and Felix Guattari, *A Thousand Plateaus: Capitalism and Schizophrenia*, (Minneapolis: University of Minnesota Press, 1987), 313.
2. See Deleuze and Guattari, *A Thousand Plateaus*, 445.
3. Georges Bataille, "je mens…" in *Hyperion*.
4. Nick Land, *The Thirst for Annihilation: Georges Bataille and Virulent Nihilism* (London: Routledge, 1992), 205.
5. Michel Serres, *Detachment* (Athens: Ohio University Press, 1989), 57-8.
6. For example, see: Meister Eckhart, *The Complete Mystical Works of Meister Eckhart* (Freiburg im Breisgau: Herder & Herder, 2009), 285.
7. Deleuze and Guattari, *A Thousand Plateaus*, 253.
8. Land, *The Thirst for Annihilation*, 28.
9. Deleuze and Guattari, *A Thousand Plateaus*, 246.
10. J.G. Ballard, "The Terminal Beach" in *The Complete Short Stories: Volume 2* (New York: Fourth Estate, 2011), 39.
11. Antonin Artaud, *The Theatre and Its Double* (New York: Grove Press, 1958), 15.
12. Jean Baudrillard, *Fatal Strategies* (Los Angeles: Semiotext(e), 2008), 47.
13. Maurice Blanchot, *The Infinite Conversation* (Minneapolis: University of Minnesota Press, 1993), 259.
14. *Ccru Writings 1997-2003*, (No Place: Time Spiral Press, 2015), 146
15. Cergat, *Earthmare: The Lost Book of Wars*, (Terra Incognita: Gnome Books, 2017), xiv-xv.
16. Blanchot, *The Infinite Conversation*, 116.
17. Georges Bataille, *Visions of Excess: Selected Writings, 1927-1939* (Minneapolis: University of Minnesota Press, 2004), 221.
18. Jean Baudrillard, *Cool Memories* (London: Verso, 1990), 70.
19. Deleuze and Guattari, *A Thousand Plateaus*, 549.

20. Michel Serres, *The Parasite* (Baltimore: John Hopkins University Press, 1982), 185.

21. Deleuze and Guattari, *A Thousand Plateaus*, 326.

22. Eckhart, *The Complete Mystical Works*, 466.

23. Baudrillard, *Cool Memories*, 36.

24. Fernando Pessoa, *The Book of Disquiet* (London: Penguin Books, 2003), 209.

25. Matthew Arnold, "Dover Beach".

26. Jean Baudrillard, *The Vital Illusion* (New York: Columbia University Press, 2000), 67.

27. Fredric Jameson, "Postmodernism and the City" in Ed. Clive Cazeaux, *The Continental Aesthetics Reader* (London: Routledge, 2000), 288.

28. Gilles Deleuze, *Difference and Repetition* (New York: Columbia University Press, 1994), 56.

29. Georges Bataille, *The Accursed Share Volumes II & III* (New York: Zone Books, 1991), 217.

30. Franco 'Bifo' Berardi, *Heroes: Mass Murder and Suicide* (London: Verso, 2015), 206-7

31. Philip K. Dick, "Survey Team" in *Second Variety: Volume Two of The Collected Stories of Philip K. Dick* (London: Gollancz, 1999), 369.

32. Philip K. Dick, "Second Variety" in *Second Variety: Volume Two of The Collected Stories of Philip K. Dick*, 27.

33. Francois Laruelle, *On the Black Universe: In the Humanistic Foundations of Color*: http://www.recessart. org/wp-content/uploads/Laruelle-Black-Universe1.pdf

34. Nick Land, *Phyl-Undhu* (No Place: Time Spiral Press, 2014), 52.

35. Franco 'Bifo' Berardi, "Biopolitics and Connective Mutation" in *Culture Machine* Vol. 7 2005.

36. Anthony Sciscione, "Symptomatic Horror: Lovecraft's 'The Colour Out of Space'" in *Leper Creativity: Cyclonopedia Symposium* (New York: Punctum Books, 2012), 132.

37. Julia Kristeva, *Powers of Horror: An Essay on Abjection* (New York: Columbia University Press, 1982), 191.

38. Jacques Derrida, *The Gift of Death* (Chicago: The University of Chicago Press, 1995), 100.

39. Gilles Deleuze, *The Logic of Sense* (New York: Columbia University Press, 1990), 153.

40. Jean Baudrillard, *Why Hasn't Everything Already Disappeared?* (London: Seagull Books, 2009), 28.

41. Jacques Derrida, *Psyche: Inventions of the Other, Vol I* (Stanford: Stanford University Press, 2007), 138-9.

42. Alexander R. Galloway and Eugene Thacker, *The Exploit: A Theory of Networks* (Minneapolis: University of Minnesota Press, 2007), 87.

43. Bataille, *The Accursed Share Volumes II & III*, 378.

44. Bataille, *Visions of Excess*, 101.

45. Baudrillard, *Cool Memories*, 107.

46. Jean Baudrillard, *Seduction* (Montréal: Ctheory Books, 2001), 172.

THE MEET

Forget your domestic hellscapes, mocked-up
Cerberus guarding the gallery, your fake drama of inter-
personal relationships (gone right, gone wrong, gone forever and here look at my tears), your righteously themed
group show at Museum Moderner Kunst Stiftung
Ludwig or GRIMM or wherever, your consumer products wryly critiquing (yet knowingly failing to extricate
themselves from) consumerism's totality, your milieu
of motorised CCTV cameras following (and by impli-
cation implicating) visitors and non-visitors alike, your
performative action in and around Halle für Kunst
Steiermark spotlighting the normally invisible thereby
subverting the installation's intended audience network,
your exploded installation view of everywhere at once for
a one-time-only fee, your found objects spanning several
decades and continents foregrounding the latest inequi-
table distribution at Ordet Milan, your architectural interventions, your inflatable dispositif, your Bermondsey
White Cube glowing liverish yellow, your 1000 Barbie
dolls melted into one another to form a semi-amor-
phous fluidity in a bum's hotel in Hollywood, your cli-
matic calamity condensed into microscopic dioramas of
the Amazon rainforest constructed on a million match

heads at the 16th Istanbul Biennial, your precarious
future interweaving inkjet prints of human anatomies
enflamed with every modern disease, your sites of civil
unrest, your open laptops showing YouTube tutorials
for male mastectomies, your international conflicts captured on 16mm film organised across four gallery spaces
livestreamed from an artificial biome, your resonates
with any fucking thing, your mirrorings, your gestures,
your flaccid seductions, your arid grindings, your brains
glued back together, your no more patriarchal constructs
as patriarchal construct, your moral givens at the always gushing teat of idiocy, your identity as anything,
your self-satisfied impermanence, your ambiguous light,
your putrid assemblages, your micro-p philosophies,
your non-linear subversions, your interior/exterior gush,
your kinetic flatulence, your tokenistic Rilke-fawning,
your reincarnated adulations, your retrospectives in
the light of whatever, your hijacking and scrambling an
audience's mobile tech to heighten their perceptivity of
the supernatural, your defanging madness via clinical
diagnostics, your explorations of cringe through a pan-
oply of wired devices, your animating algorithm, your
watermarked stock photos of pregnant bellies and defor-
ested mud, your old hat old head at the New Museum
in New York, your finance district's working class poor
eating their own shit in Toronto, your complex poetic
forms made from formulaic poesies, your beadwork joy,
your capitalist magic, your repurposed gall bladders
of every eminent critic, your explicitly fantastical solo
show of open-doored fridges at Ginny on Frederick,
your video screens filling the entirety of anything, your

robotic fear of snakes as regenerative at Sprüth Magers, your exhibition's shifting textures described as hesitant or melancholy or both, your malignant Western undertones, your truly transformative experience as research or rigour, your transformed waste as witchcraft in Los Angeles, your fierce undercurrent of, your bleaker stirrings, your multitude of distressed and abraded materials, your molluscs as metaphors, your uncanny beauty of mass-produced materials, your ruination as inspiration, your so-so singular vision of societal collapse, your interspecies collaborations, your apocalyptic impact gone soft, your photosensitive sheets, your orgiastic melding of baby heads, your indefinable something, your content developed using speculative methodologies, your apparatus by proxy, your art as purpose or ethics, your body of work that asks us to care, your intergenerational seepage, your mediated spaces as archives that warp, your dead families drawn from grainy photographs, your pushing the efficacy of your caged animals as symbols, your metres of servo motors, sensors and semiconductors sheathed in a reflective 3D-printed skin, your experiments with bacteria, your sheets of aluminium treated with a wash of roseate acrylic, your convergence and divergence and spoon-fed intelligence, your tubular lengths of PVC, your global curatorial reach, your diminished impact due to cross-cultural adaptation, your electrically powered rods endlessly hitting a surface… and so forget your drugged dream of buying yourself a human when humans just want to watch TV, forget your alienation, your monotony, your anxiety, forget the ageless intimacy of the art it induces, the literal and metaphorical potential of your visitors' insides, your unintentional themes, your candid toxicity, your car-boot triennial, your surgery as provocation, your damp interiors, your growing bodies in a lake in the courtyard of MoMA PS1, your sly eschewal of documentation, your self-actualising as this new paintbrush, your psilocybin-induced soul-searching, your landfills covered in foraging deer, your synthetic life forms slithering under WetLab doors on Governors Island, your audacious disruptions of today's digitally interconnected world, your uncompromising video sculpture of unstill lives, your zombie formalism as the new pop art, your looking so-so cool on Instagram, your flattened trompe l'oeil, your defining your practice in relationship to whatever, your throwing up outside Cuchifritos Gallery at the fake severed heads nailed to its triangular pediment, your post-internet tactility disappeared down chimeric peepholes, your prismatic logo in a druggy swamp of looney tune hybridity, your new ways of understanding humanity through the miracle of economic benevolence, your thematic parameter of atemporality, your extinction notes overlaid with perforated cartoons, your retrofitted motivations, your celebrity murders, your photoshopping of the world without you, your flippable film-objects, your displaced cultural capital in an anonymous signature style, your supercharged connoisseurship of art's illimitable data as gorged iridescence, your Frankenstein's monster in a good way, your bullshit collaboration with an alien species, because we know because that's what we are and because you are not us.

We are *courtesy the artists.*

We will make staying alive seem like a dare. We offer you an object representative of the conditions that expunged our identities, a sci-fi-horror-true-crime-text-as-exhibition, if you will. We offer you the way too real. You'll remember when your arsehole went and everything else followed. Our project is not merely multigenerational or multicultural, but multidimensional – multifaceted beyond your current capacity for faceting. We plan on cratering brains, whole heads. We have no lessons about isolation or togetherness or anything else. We're not here to inform but to destroy – a beautiful devastation, an analgesic insurrection. We are not of you or for you but in front of you – as inevitable as your final thought and equally thrilling. You need us to move things along; you're getting nowhere on your own. Put your trust in us: we are your companion species for the end. We would like to thank our donors, sponsors and supporters, who must, for now at least, remain anonymous.

Couldn't we feed exhibition-goers into the installation, worldwide across every major gallery in the world, so that by the time its effects become clear it's too late to do anything about it?

Do we even need them to understand it? Remember what Lawrence Weiner said: "Once you know about a work of mine you own it. There's no way I can climb inside someone's head and remove it." Once we get ours in their heads it'll spread like a stroke, a fungus, a bushfire, and there'll be no taking it out without removing the brain altogether. Nothing left to take. Can't extract a cavity. The vicissitudes of decay, of explosive materials. This text-based work.

I take 300gms of Nortriptyline and sleep. I sleep industrially idiosyncratic reliquaries of whatever it is a god sleeps.

A man is shouting in the street. He has a revelation to share, same one he shares every day. A rough translation:

...You hear me? You hear me? You have girls? You all have girls. You can't hide them. Not from God. You can't hide them from God. Nobody hides from God. They are holy, but you don't understand. Holy and holely (lifts his arms as if in praise for 'holy' and makes holes with his thumbs and forefingers for 'holey'), get it? God is in them, see. He has fingers everywhere. They're full of holes. God's hands and fingers, all his fingers in them. He makes them dance. Without God they're all just holes. Holy is holey. They have holes for God. You can't protect them. You can't make them dance. You fake and take and hate. Listen to your girls before it's too late. Listen, your ears are holes. Be holy. Be holy. God has fingers for you all. You hear me? You hear me?

We tell him we support his art. We commend his performative truth. He asks us to show our hands, turn the fingers into holes. We raise our arms up and wave our voided digits above our heads like we have seen the light and are now ecstatically blind to everything else. We become his disciples for as long as it amuses us, then retreat from the window.

There was a man who died. Someone gagged him, tied him up and cut his hands off. He bled out for however long it took, and was found the next morning by his half-sister, flown in from Helsinki for a long weekend. I'd returned to London on the day it happened. And so what, right? A population of 9 million plus, could have been anyone. But then it wasn't of any of them that he had hundreds of photographs on his phone, it was me, and they'd be coming to find out why. The lunchtime news was full of it, and while this detail about the photographs had been kept from the press, I knew they were there, knew he'd been following me, had observed him for the past month or so feigning nonchalant scrolling as he amassed this supposedly candid pictorial record of someone feigning a life right back at him.

I was opening my door when I noticed someone beside me, breathing heavy, leaning into me. I hadn't seen them approach, and the sudden appearance shit me up. Can I come in? Let me in! Quick! Things progressed from there, and now this.

I ran back out onto the street, looked up at the house opposite, and there at a first-floor window was a face. Up ahead a woman in a black van looking up at the same window, and signals being exchanged. I crossed the road, took a left turn down a narrow alleyway backing on to dozens of shabby-looking gardens. There was no one about, so I …

What the fuck?

What the fuck what?

What the fuck are you talking about?

Something happened to me. I'm telling you. It's not safe, people know. The authorities, whoever.

This is isn't a thriller.

I think it is, I really think it is.

It's not.

It might be.

There was Acker, I suppose. Her search for a sprawl-ing, inclusive identity: inserting her "I" into other writ-er's texts. Who knows what the rejection of identity does to texts, what gets inserted, what taken away. What the texts then become.

She's on the zombie formalism thing again, said Uta, not looking up from her laptop.

Who? replied Gogo, standing on his head, Who am I? Who am I?

Hoptman, said Uta, louder now, exasperated.

Who? I said, with Gerhard, like we were the same person.

Laura Hoptman, MoMA curator, you know. She's in *Art in America*. Here, listen: "We're hanging on the next new thing. What if that's not the way it's working anymore? What if there is no next new thing? Do we sit around and mourn the fact that we've seen it before? There's a way to look at creativity that doesn't necessar-ily have to do with creating something we've never seen before. It can be about reinterpreting or misinterpreting the world that's already around us."

She's not wrong, said Gerhard.

She will be, I said. Fucking zombie-eater will chew on her well-observed defeatism.

Maybe she should be the first to go, said Uta. We could film it.

You look like you've been made by Berlinde De Bruyckere, said Uta, you know, kind of unfinished, kind of headless.

Gogo smiled, laughed, started to piss. Uta watched it run up Gogo's body to the floor, soaking the front of their T-shirt, flooding the eyes, pooling around the hair.

Didn't someone do all 533 of Edouard Levé's *Oeuvres* projects at Art Basel or something?

They must have done. How long has it been?

Remind me, was it any good?

You fucking kidding?

Yeah.

Artists who don't make art are perverts, and we were perverted as they come. Our art gig now was as fugitives, asexual sci-fi B-movie Martian couturiers of human brains. Artists as monsters. Sadistic, criminal, anti-homo-sapien-pro-homo wunderkinds. The dematerialisation of art needed a process worthy of itself, not more anartist schtick, not the desacralisation of what was already utterly divested of all religious content, save the fucking of innocents which would never be over. Art history wonks made proper wonky with seeing, we take any disruption of the viewership we can get, but there are limits: limits to the limits themselves, to the plausible transgression of what isn't there. We are emblematic of an exhaustive knowledge seeming to morph into ignorance. Come on! No more kinetic uses of colour that aren't the entire frosty-slurping audience being sick over each other. If your recent work is to be placed in the context of your earlier groundbreaking projects, shouldn't something be falling over by now? If 3-D scanners and printers won't put the sculptors to bed, it's left to us. About eight/nine years ago there were reports of spray-painted poodles torn to pieces in the now defunct Toronto artspace, Videofag. They were just reports.

I once pissed myself at the Hirshorn. Still getting used to this body and there it was. I remember being surrounded by shellacked mega-trucks, but I could be making that up. It was an Art Forum Must See. I'd written a screamer in my head, something like *Art: it's not a question of money anymore*, and then it was too late.

It's easy done. I pissed myself in the Micheline Szwajcer Gallery, Antwerp, or was it the MuHKA. The sun was on my legs and I didn't notice right away. Oh and in Hua International Beijing as well, and Kraftwerk, Berlin.

We should launch our own gallery: First on Venus (Rotten Pinocchios, Till Dresden, Transformers, whatever) will debut at the wherever as part of whatever, organised by whomever, a former assistant curator at a prestigious museum would be good, to open later this year.

Get ourselves a former Fitzrovia haberdashery. A derelict basement, flooded even, upstairs a series of small, unprepossessing rooms. Convert it into a 4,000 sq. ft. gallery, host other galleries on a biannual basis. The first incumbent could be a searing exploration of identity, sexuality, beauty, and the fragility of existence. Imagine the contrast when we present our wares.

Too London-centric.

Uta is reading from the death of someone on Instagram: spent his life covering the Berlin arts scene, sucked cocks up his shitter like a hoover, famous for an acerbic wit, even laughs at own suicide.

Has to be Frieze week, right?

So cold in October.

Don't piss yourself, you'll be fine.

Can we be post- something? Are we art from the gut or the head?

To be posthumanist you have to be human first, right?

Installation view of Gogo's colon.

I pissed myself in Schinkel Pavillon, in Museo De Arte Miguel Urrutia, Bogotá, Dortmunder Kunstverein, Carbon 12, Dubai, and in the Albright-Knox Art Gallery in Buffalo.

We're not doing that anymore.

We've done the pissing ourselves thing.

At the Pompidou? At the Louvre?

Was it a painterly stain?

A hot button issue played out to the sound of a slow-turning millstone from Dreyer's *Vampyr*?

An impassioned show.

An emotionally charged extravaganza of visceral honesty and vulnerability.

A paleoclimatological found footage from hundreds of millions of years ago. We could construct a false continuum in the edit. We could make it about humans.

Found footage of Gogo's colon.

Fuck me if your fascinating details just aren't fascinating.

It's hard to say, because I've no idea what I'm talking about.

Performative photographs of ethereal monsters for the post-internet age.

A giant petri dish growing subcultures that will one day redeem society.

Killer doses of retrofuturism, of intergalactic horseshit.

Beautifully wrong hyperrealist supermax.

Aggressively pruned high entropy nerdcore

Can we call it *I Wept the Night You Left and Now Everyone Else is Just Weather*?

Can we Frieze LA in midsummer?

Can we put emergency-room swing doors on a meth lab?

Can we start a new world war?

Camouflage is so camp.

What next? Car accidents? Plane crashes? Suicides? We in 1963 already?

Who was it said artists own themselves like academics own italics?

Nobody.

Can we have mirrored plexiglass torsos? Can we at least be sliced and spliced like Warhol? Day and night Dior. Dior forever.

Can we shoot each other?

If we had our own media company we could produce content for mass consumption. Draw them in with fluff and then choke them to death.

Can we become products?

Our work could explore the current preponderance of neoliberal gadgetry, freshly hatched head trips for some digital pastiche of reality, colonial crimes as domestic homicides, a see-sawing monumentality of mimesis, our leisure burden oh so urgently rendered.

A glut of nebbish influencers experience previously unseen brand of dysphoria.

No archival dimension: colliding planets do not keep records.

I quote: I don't think any artist today can afford for their work to be divorced from their biography.

Kill all social documentarians.

Artist as cipher. Art as cranial Semtex. Final word. Endgame.

Can we just be flippant for once?

They all laugh, only it sounds like screeching machinery, like tropical birds fed slowly, tail-first into an industrial mincer.

Can't work out if we're anti- or pro-.

So anti- we've looped, become pro- through erasure. But pro- what?

Pro-revolt, pro-revolting, so revolting we're gorgeous again.

Like Juan Rivero.

If you want.

In various states of unflesh

You know I once got kicked out of Arebyte for asking too many questions. Same thing at Seventeen. Bent the assistant's ear into a club foot. I wanted to know why I should care. *She Keeps Me Damn Alive* was on: I shot everything that moved. I gamified my indifference. I said, I come toting no fucks and I need you to enlighten me. Did you find it immersive? she asked. I mean, I'm a cipher, a nobody, I find every-fucking-thing immersive, I said. What was I gonna say?

Maybe ours should be a LARP.

Is this one long vamp, or are we heading somewhere?

One thing before we start.

We haven't started yet?

Do you think my Replika loves me?

Sure, why not.

At the risk of repeating ourselves, we embrace inertia.

Resurrect more gooey exhortations holding errant lovers to account.

More AbEx horror films cut with decapitated bodies in skinnies and nipple-clamps.

Creepy voices and neurosurgeries, Chronic Fatigue Syndrome of trophy spouses chain-smoking away the trippy boredom of the exurbs.

Diaristic force of wilted Walmart still lifes.

Algorithmic autopoiesis of alcoholic isolation and excessive screen time.

The other-than-human legibility of orgiastic, asemic flurries fed into a supercomputer at the University of Texas.

Manchild's self-portrait of murdered lovers wrapped in old carpet.

Shot using pink Uzi.

Golden Kalashnikov.

Sociopolitical freebase for the post-industrial human spirit.

McCarthy's *Human Object* used as sex toy by Carly Rae Summers.

Inscrutable narratives captured by security cameras on the haunted houses of an imagined American heartland.

Are we emerging or mid-career?

Well, we're not Happy Meal toys in painted bronze made to dwarf the Statue of Unity if that's what you mean.

It wasn't.

The carrier bag theory of art pulled tight over your head till it's all over.

If we induce strokes, can they at least have gestural intensity?

We can say anything and they'll come. Aesthetic aneurisms guaranteed. QR coding body parts transferring ownership to the Institute of Plastination with immediate effect. Art so routinely overpromises on its ability to arrive at its own bleeding edge, who's going to believe a thing we say?

A witch hunt-cum-multi-venue exhibition: MASS MoCA has sixteen acres and fourteen buildings for artists to lose their shit in. Who'd notice four more?

Impasto layers of sex workers wrapped in plastic.

Lurid renditions of raw meat as commentary on the mutable nature of human identity.

Willem de Kooning said he wanted to paint like Ingres and Soutine at the same time.

How many things can we do at once?

I can paint with my cunt in your mouth.

No vaccinations required to enter our consensual reality.

My composition of skinned crocodiles radiates a garish, exotic energy.

My digital onslaught is almost unbearable, nearly sublime.

VR goggles render an alien mood at Mizuma & Kips.

A series of luminous green centipedes, each the size of large stretching cats, rest on satin cushions distributed throughout the vaulted cellar of the Alexander Battery at Helsinki Biennial on Vallisaari Island. Visitors to the exhibit are frequently attacked and some have had to be rescued from the underground space by armed officials. CGI glyphs and squiggles combine with a scratchy soundscape of high-pitched synthetic beeps and futuristic collections of gory dioramas and tablescapes to suggest a conglomerated web of nonhuman agency.

Donna Haraway is proper multisensory. She calls it *tentacular thinking*. And yet, more flailing amputees.

So far we're Cnidarians missing our cnidocytes. We're a stuttering lab experiment, a demented proto-science, a goofy killing squad, disconnected, diffractive rationales going no-fucking-where.

A delightfully ambiguous arts program all too easily mistaken for a death cult.

Are we doing the intertitles for our biopic already?

A seemingly prescient proposal for an apocalyptic interspecies encounter consisting of Color Field paintings in crocheted frames smashed over the heads of spectators in some Marx Brothers take on kinetic avant-gardism.

A form of hybrid warfare deploying various synthetic media to articulate nihilistic decriminalisation strategies for the future of all genuine provocation.

Did I happen upon the MIT Center for Advanced Virtuality? Or in other words…

Please stop.

Quite.

Quite why we should, I don't know. Silence ain't so fucking pretty, am I wrong?

I'm not interested in an artist's feelings.

Disinterest has its own paraphernalia.

Slide n Shred à la Carsten Höller à la Poe.

This or that iteration of this or that.

Art as a model for the lag in your imminent death and impending obsolescence at CAMP, Miami.

A seminal indoctrination congeals in the slippery and unexplained landscapes to shore us up against forgetting.

Arresting back-lit tondos of anti-scapes, round and treacherous, muddled nowheres that feel all too familiar, cumulative effects that consternate the linear.

Bricoleurs deconstructing the tortured machismo of limp dicks and impossibly congested intestines.

Need spontaneous forms with a deeply emotional impact.

We need the right media, and something anyone can get.

Who can afford to be abstruse?

Cronyism for the masses.

Our art will die from exposure.

This art destroys its host.

Pejoratively likened to a digital grimoire.

Art requires contextualisation to be reprehensible.

Our glitch oeuvre.

Marginalised people mounted on the wall alongside air conditioners, aural texture of subjects' testimonial recordings.

I'm building an environment for optimal absorption with SketchUp.

A structured space within which unpredictable artistic outcomes can emerge.

Anti-anthropocentric philosophies create edible specimens, abstract human effigies, inimitable motifs.

Their period-appropriate human surface, in a capacious sense, stretched around a tall wooden armature.

Still not picturing it.

Problematic dynamics of objectification.

The scanning apps aren't capturing the basic polarities: blurred visuals, conflicting strains, increasingly confused threats to our own wellbeing.

Synergistic self-contamination.

Someone close that window, turning cyanotype here.

What is it when even our diversions become fractured?

Pioneering receptor ambiguities at the MoCADA… can we concentrate?

What do we even have so far?

An ungainly tetraptych of some canonically expansive execution pyre.

Using the piss-stain method.

A preoccupation with some speculative human/nonhuman collaboration with an as yet undefined transformative potential.

The transubstantiation of pissed pants.

An expedited desensitisation…

Followed by an immediate enhancement of all human sensitivities…

To superhuman levels…

Kaboom!

I love Cornell's obsessiveness, but his sentimentality disgusts me. Much too reverent of memory, all those human connections: yuck!

Could we create a box that destroys memory and human connectivity?

Now that would be a thing.

You know how Warhol brought the dead back to life? Well, why not do the opposite of that? You know, if the difference between art and life is not a visual difference, then what if the difference between the living and the dead wasn't visual either?

Philosophical zombies, you mean?

Wasn't Andy one of those?

I mean, could we eradicate all human experience and leave everything intact?

How is that the answer?

I'm not sure yet.

We won't know till we've made it; making it will give us the tools to understand.

This is some painful shit.

I think it needs to be. It doesn't seem to work any other way.

I blame Andy's ugly-arse nose for all this.

Big old pores. He had the skin shaved off, but it didn't work.

Made it worse. Should have gone full rhinoplasty.

We could call ourselves Andy Warhol's Rhinoplasty.

Well, it's kind of the opposite of embodied meaning: the embodied absence of meaning.

Wouldn't the opposite be disembodied non-meaning, disembodied nonsense?

But the humans would be disembodied, wouldn't they? There'd be nowhere for their consciousness to exist.

Didn't Danto say something about wakeful dreams being important?

Sure, and the opposite of that would be a sleeping life.

So the P-zombies are like Pod people?

Kind of, yeah.

We have a purely apophatic vision of what art should be and we're not afraid to use it.

We don't need to kill anyone, just put holes in them. Perforate them.

Make them leaky and porous, kind of disintegrated.

I think we should change our name to Stab Frenzy.

I like it.

Do you think we could get Bjarne Melgaard to redesign the moon?

Before we blow it up.

He could do our throne for after as well.

There was that mathematician advocated for the destruction of the moon.

Alexander Abian: he's my fucking hero.

Crazy mathematicians are the absolute best.

So fuckable.

We gots to end the world's virginity.

With our spiky oversized genitals.

I bring up an image of Olga Kroytor looking so hot and dead and alive in her open grave in 2013. But I have nothing to say. Our doomscrolling snarled into puppies and more puppies.

For *The retrospective view of the pathway*, Roger Hiorns spent twenty-six years burying passenger aircraft.

I think he presents an alternative history of flight.

Generations to come will think we flew through the earth.

Or that we got so bored with ourselves we consecrated modes of transport.

Buried our crucifixions.

Who's this "we"?

What…? I'm in character.

We could deepfake the end of the world. A video of the near-future.

Premier at the Biennale Matter of Art in Prague.

Have it leak onto the major news channels.

No one's gonna believe that.

The wheel of art turned and turned and made us puke, gave us the shits. We scraped against all the many caricaturists of bafflement and fetish, the circus animals trying to work out what it is to be human. Without me they were a scalene piercing a puppy dog. We'd cultivated a botched frivolity, an anecdotal, slinky artificialism. Landless remains of what it meant to be ardent.

What's a gerund we can own? Our very own neologism.

You mean like videos of teenagers jumping off cliffs?

Ice cream parlours and arcades, all kinds of off places to fuck.

Anticipate the worst confessional.

Sacrificial twinks and twirly girls toying with startling juxtapositions of …

All your pronouns are indecent. Toyen knew. Call me sad male maker of poisons, said Uta.

The history of found objects is so many flags in shit.

The silk stockings under my trousers are all ladders.

I have a horror connoisseur's paradisiacal clairvoyance.

What do you see?

I see you turning up to our opening garbed in horrific vulvas.

Can I wear my space suit?

Oooo my interiority's all atremor.

Do you believe my sadness or what?

I believe in our immediate and saturating commercial success.

I believe in Bataille's *informe* and the rejuvenating properties of day-old kestrel piss.

WOW re unfinished documentary about a massacre.

About a madman.

WOW re images of sandblasted human organs sewn onto empty pillowcases.

Inchoate heads melted into enigmatic genital forms: WOW or no?

WOW overkill WOW characters and issues, humanising tendencies exacerbated by suffocating normalcy. Black snowmen in the daadgalerie, Berlin.

Dayglo graffito of a dissected fetus at Ramekin Crucible on the Lower East Side.

What is it even worth doing to these creatures?

The most charismatic fictionalisation of self-portraiture ever committed to film.

Sooo achingly umbilical.

Can we wreak terrible havoc upon the world already?

I sniff a vaguely po-mo pattern to all this.

Don't pathologise my tchotchkes; I need me shiny, brightly coloured plastics to choke to death on.

Is there some site-specificity to our limitless imagination?

You want to leave already?

What if we've become inoperably human? You ever think of that?

I'm all bags of coal and string.

Histories of disappearance, architectures of violence.

Ferocious in the interstices.

I draw inspiration from mobile phone footage of furry beatings and grieving mothers.

Tell me what it is we're interrogating.

Undifferentiated difference, folds in the conditional, impolite tenderness.

The aftermath of a crime.

Twocked motors all sticky with pedestrians.

And there she sits, uninterested in aligning with any current styles, imperiously obscure.

Where is our monograph coming from?

Some drunks somewhere, unrestrained neo-symbolists in a basement churning out samizdat exclusives for sale at Camden Market.

Portrait of the artist wearing a niqab and left by the side of the road to choke on diesel fumes.

Stroboscopic portrait of the artist as reinvigorated cliché – twenty-four times every second.

Ravenous, bloodshot portrait of a chem trail from a ceiling fan.

Scrunched up cramming of irregular cells into this awkward art pose.

Praise be to all our gauzy inquisitors.

Blessed are those whose suffering is special.

Obviate much?

The evocation of anti-societal fervour in yet another blue-chip gallery.

Fractious till I die.

I blame my pervasively heteronormative upbringing. It's all there in my files.

Aren't we facing persecution and oppression from all sides?

The humans are so proud of being humans.

Where do we start with their fuckedupness?

There isn't even a word for what we have to do.

Makes it hard to talk about, I guess.

I refuse to get psyched about a TikTok of some Japanese teen taking a shit in Derek Jarman's garden under the title *Arse Ejected Death Syndrome*.

Fucking maladroit.

Miscellaneous agitprop.

Agitpoop.

My shit would circle the entire fucking planet.

Its length an index of our combined disaffection.

We unite behind your faeces.

Your doctrinaire irreverence.

Poop=Death collective.

Girth and stench a metric of our terrible love.

Dungeness is cool, though; like a Lopushansky film. We could do something there.

Continued commodification of the dystopian seaside.

Scungy Dungy.

Sprawling, predatory horror at Luxembourg & Dayan.

Everywhere I go I'm accompanied by a conservator: haughty type, Harvard boy, stupid-rich, diamond-encrusted motherfucker. We ooh and aah at wall-mounted assemblages of monochromatic screens radiating toxic light from some sun-bleached intestine of LA. We plunge into an essayistic montage of scabrous dialogues and testimonies, weird dioramas populated by wealthy art

collectors, eloquent meth-heads and the bloated corpses
of Theresa Duncan and Jeremy Blake.

Of all the disquieting muses, Valerie Solanas really
mashes my fibres. She's the catalyst of stage-2 Andy – cut-up
Andy (SCUM manifesto, in light of original acronymic periods, enacted by proxy) – but it doesn't stop there: I could
watch her in *I, a Man* and *Bike Boy* till my eyes bleed.

I ran my fast fashion art-group, Hinterland, from a
former slaughterhouse in Madrid. We all had gold laptops and hands and necks inked by Dr Woo. Art that
operated anywhere near the limits of human knowledge
was our immediate target: a sustained campaign of as-
perity, of coldblooded ridicule. But all too brief, all too
incandescent. We once dropped pulpy, dramaturgically
dubious materials from decommissioned military aircraft over the American heartland. Don't ask why; it
didn't matter. Some accused us of inveigling pre-cine-
matic allegories into a knotty tryst with post-cinematic,
geopolitical clusterfucks.

I'm coming from a generation of pregnant bodies, if
you will. The last mother, the one I'm tempted to own
(my Midwich host), internalised this here disembodiment, reassembled a general lack of human connection
like her womb was working in digital collage. A kind of
act of mummification, if you will. Shit, someone's got to
be the first black, non-binary, non-human, art-terrorist
nobody of the year.

The first subjects were different states of… you know,
dismissed as embarrassing.

Problem is they want everything.

And then we're censored for ugliness.

The past is fragile like that.

This new documentary on surgically enhanced gender roles looks great.

Young women flaunting bodies on social media as if belly button fluff and ingrowing toenails were a different world.

We're changelings. Our fairy godmother's a xenomorph. We become aware of ourselves in a disarranged way.

Give me the apocalypse or give me snarling scenesters in Jurassic Park T-shirts drinking molten aluminium.

We consider that offensive east of the Hudson.

Different experiences won't take you beyond consumerism.

Jeffrey Deitch spoke to me in a dream. He seemed like he was into what we were doing, but he was talking Somali. Then Larry Gagosian turned up shouting all kinds of angry shit in Tamil. I end up at HOME in Chinatown. I quaff way too much champagne and experience moments of menacing intimacy. I will end up idiosyncratically integrating them to ironic aesthetic effect.

Gogo contemplates their material dregs recurved into a hard belly.

Uta tells them their dick is the sculptural equivalent of dinosaurs in paradise.

This reciprocal vulnerability is just disillusioned cognoscenti getting all touchy-feely.

A mixture of parodic reference and comedic nihilism.

A 10ft dead narcissus with limbs and a dick sited in the JAX District, Saudi Arabia.

I've noticed the more vulnerable we get, the better we –

Ha, listen: Vulnerability is a necessary precursor to transformation.

I regard this as our tacit invitation.

And they say Horror's reactionary.

Even in flashes I'm too long for this world.

Oddly disembodied flat forms at the Tutu Gallery through February.

In 1882, Van Gogh was into rubbish in a big way. Told God it was beautiful.

All true believers in the religion of art dig crap.

It's that art as alchemy thing. The aestheticising hand or eye.

Who ever thought God was this anthropomorphised canine with its eyes stabbed out?

Everything becomes useless when it becomes art.

Work at the intersection of horror, contemporary art, and boredom is what you'd do if your head exploded in the mirror and you were still there, watching.

It's extremely mundane, but also the worst thing ever.

It's much more complicated than it can be.

If someone was trying to kill me, I'd brush my hair. That's so utterly ridiculous, right?

The horror genre needs people like you. All you need do is see yourself exist.

Art21 at NeueHouse, NYC is where things don't seem to add up. Stuff goes wrong every time.

I love that he doesn't stay away.

I love doodling with the end of the world.

I love doodling with the end of art.

Same thing.

I love writing fan fiction with my teeth.

We are doodling, this is doodling – the equivalent of doodling with our vocal cords.

Do we have to spell it out?

The antagonistic properties of profane idols are the too quick rearrangement of birds in a bomb blast.

Need gigantic test site for our landmark orgasm.

A routine comedy routine featuring people gasses and artificial postures.

Uta does the burst tongue act: the closed-mouth cough, pupils like balled-up knickers in a washing machine.

Is this what it is to be a shell of myself?

Is a dimensionless seeing really the description I'm looking for?

I feel like so many tunnels in jelly.

Well don't.

I've taken to flushing my expectations by the dozen.

Well don't.

Blood shows you mean it.

Can a selfhood be padded with new suicides?

We'd make terrible engineers.

We need something like a conventional comb for thoughts.

I once ground down ibex horn and poured it into aspirin shells.

I put the longest strand of unbroken sense data in a big square device.

I forgot my body was attached.

Who volunteers to have their shame scattered in a frozen universe?

Who dropped Hitler on his head?

On Margate sands… and all that.

Nothing with nothing.

Let's not remind ourselves of her, poor thing.

Our deliquescing martyr of the sands.

She'd like that.

My code of ethics is horizontal.

Hate is nutritive.

Masseurs-turned-stranglers administering lightning bolts to monkeys.

You know there's a committee in Geneva on the use of art as a weapon.

I'm trying to think of the word for when you can't think of a word and it's driving you fucking crazy and it's driving me fucking crazy.

The old onomatomania loop.

Gogo gushing about how our conjugated brain mass will one day resemble finely sliced fruitcake.

All of us shocked at how the shock of the spontaneous is such a shocking snooze.

So there are these weird burrowing creatures trying to translate a swan's meow and not one of them has a fucking clue.

If you're sticking your head in, you need to lubricate the cow.

Enough slippery already, build a tank, chew a hole.

We a literal borehole.

We're numbing the subject.

There should be more integration of plant-life and beautiful kids.

See them anytime you want, high on glitter, reproducing in Echo Park after Sherrie Levine.

Such awful chemicals these days. Rip a young nose clean off.

An inch of falsetto for a lifetime of reality.

We gonna need a stenographer for all these subplots.

Uta is moistening the prongs of several plugs inside her mouth. She says that peonies fed on blood turn transparent at the edges, but no one believes her.

I'm too busy rehearsing my waterboard face to consider the truth of anything.

We need more on the cuttability of creepy fluids.

Noises of exaggerated disbelief. Some yucky, some the sound of unwinding duct tape for whatever reason.

Another Presbyterian fakir on hallucinogens is emptying his consciousness into my feed.

I felt proper royal these past years. Had me a silvered baby. Intellect turned lingerie, all skimpy, perforated. Men would pay to lick my scrofula.

Theory is fucking loathsome.

Said all casual like. Oh and my personality is untenable, by the way.

Didn't you write about a cosmopolitan Iraq in strikethrough like you saying some shit?

We all gathered around peepholes jacking in our palms.

A questionable longitudinal relief.

We try more and more tongue, we so slurring everything like spunk running off chrome

Our Caligula all caliginous init. We way too hey this seawater almost sweet you feel me? Where our baby pink blood at? This madness got no wings.

I don't care to walk, I unlike legs.

Once Wittgenstein has run out of relatives there will be no more books.

I once grew new fingers in my sleep.

I really hate to identify, you know that, I'm no reductionist and all, but sometimes, just sometimes I has to purge this paleface condescension like: You idiot motherfucker, this chocolate got pi to a thousand decimal places, and you barely keep your mouth still when you read.

We're all extraterrestrial green now.

I'm wondering, can pure terror ever be genuinely experimental?

If anything, life must be shorter and full of love; isn't that something they say?

I'm much fonder of an asphyxiate's bulging eyes than I care to admit

Didn't you just?

People have opinions.

Vile inventions, outright darkness.

Gerhard says if we climb the walls we can put our ears to the ceiling and listen to the room above. He feels the voices are quite close.

Uta hissing like she's losing air.

I remember I could smell we all needed the toilet at once. Gogo's farts more plaintive than ours.

I've never modestly dropped a thing.

At night we gazed at videos of people sleeping as a proxy for our own unconsciousness. The grand sweep of our lives was merciless. We would never be caught begging forgiveness. The following day was yesterday, because neither one ended or began.

We see through everyone. Repulsively transparent, just all of them.

Our problem was we needed more veneers.

Uta once tried to be kind for a whole 24 hours. And all the time her meagre sense of self, a thing the size and shape of a coiled tadpole, under siege. If we could make them kind, wouldn't they disappear?

Why not catwalk the murders of Andrew Cunanan during Paris Fashion Week?

My enthusiasms dress me up.

How much prettier can a girl get?

It was absurd to not pretend. It was absurd to not pretend we were anything more than gorgeous insects, drugged-up fierce, perfectly charming, dingy eyed, bludgeoned to death by this international pressure to be injudiciously fashionable, sensitive, witty, reduced.

It's imperative to always be precisely like everybody else, tag your friends.

All that yessing's hard on the eyes.

Uta is squeezing her cesarean scar like that burger thing they do with pussies in pornos. Ain't it pretty, she says. And we all snicker as Gogo puts his penis back in his pants.

That was so like us.

Sordid Sistine.

Sordid yourself.

Hey, my brain's not some planisphere for y'all to roll around on you know. I got sensitivities here.

Where's a plenum to sit?

Standing up, feeble in her dirty yellow hair, barely able to walk, one time goddess of sleazy seaside resorts squinting at the out of season light, Uta embodied the antiproduct.

It was a moment, consolidated, GIF of a face sandblasted back to the bone.

What's more human than Bethlehem in a shoebox?

A turd covered in scar tissue.

Run the test, Deckard.

We betrayers.

How can we betray a species that isn't ours?

If we open zones of opaque offense, if we militarise this DNFing, if assassinations weren't fatal but worse than fatal, all our difficult carnivalesque anxiety, all our elliptical gossip, our heartfelt penchant for the asymmetric…

What's he on about?

What if the schizo finds out who they are?

Maybe they scream.

Maybe it's a terrified boredom.

Can't we bore them out of their minds?

What, again?

Their attention spans are so short they can almost be bored and excited at the same time.

Throw them a party.

Human parties revel in such miserable little pleasures.

Hey wait, why does Gerhard have a burnhole through the top of his head?

What's all that shit coming out?

Burnhole bumhole.

No, really, what is that?

I'm no neurobiologist, but I heard there's a certain predictability when it comes to opening brains and this ain't it.

Gogo was squatting by the door, babbling something about art as nerve agent. Their face half-closed, eyes complex somehow and faint.

Are we liquidated in the pretend? Are we fatty tissue?

Are we tarte à la crème à la devotional giggling?

Are we fuck as like.

Gerhard once had a fascinating, explosive wife. She was much less real than us with no manifest effort. Quite wonderfully insincere. Sinuous as a catwalk invertebrate, howling voice, never less than performance-ready. She once sunk her teeth in my neck. I never could figure out why. I would need to see twice as much, three, four times more than I ever did. I would need to see more than there was to see.

Nobody had a wife more hostile to introversion.

A simpering politeness, as I recall.

Unctuous beyond compare.

She once executed a pony using cybernetics. She whispered in its ear and the thing just fell to bits.

I don't think Gerhard ever had a wife.

I would be obliged to make her up.

I'm done with this excursus already.

It had all happened and we refused to believe it would keep happening. We were clinging to anarchic impersonality till we were stuck together, strained, unendurable, more humanly inhuman than we'd ever been and then... and then nothing happened, in that everything kept happening, our adversarial interruptions consumed by the target, no sabotage, no rupture, no revolting volte-face.

One creamy fucking tear is all it takes and I got this cloying PTSD for weeks. Headaches like someone poured bricks in my ear.

I once recovered from a tiny scratch. So weak, couldn't move out my bed, practically igneous. I thought I saw God. He was some kind of intelligent lard. He was a nervous disease. He was fully submersible. He told me the dead have nothing left, because they can no longer die. I admire the appetites of the dead. And I told Him so.

Something must be missing. Have we accumulated all the concrete data?

Could I have felt something without pretending to feel it?

We sat around the room not quite facing each other, decaying transparencies, our version of togetherness a discordant melody of interlocking depersonalisations. We looked because no choice at everything suspiciously, knowing that's what looking is. We checked we were still alive and we were.

Uta with her schematics of art-types prone to luxuriant paralysis – those into guns, kids, genital mutilation, involuntary euthanasia, way-too-drunk-for-safe-words-BDSM – and who could ever get enough? And yet the answer tried to come at us from nonexistent angles, what looked like a psychosis emerging from the most peripheral of realities.

I want the body I want. But I do not want to belong; I'll take all the decrements of that till I'm so emphatically othered we'll have only our difference in common. You can imagine the look he gave me, like if this isn't the weirdest break-up in history then what, degusting the peculiar flavour of every word in turn in case there remained some flimsy possibility that my severance from the world might not include him, that my spurning of gender and species and the entire fucking anthropomorphised universe left some as yet unclaimed recess where we could remain together, much as we'd been before, a place where love existed and resembled the ultimate meaning of our spatiotemporal confluence.

Hilarious. This sap have a name?

Yeah, I forget. Made a growling sound when you said it. Ceremonious tic like all the others.

It's a conspiracy every day to make me care about something. I don't, I do not care, not about any of it. I'm a streamlined processing unit of uncaring; I'm a machine of indifference. Prick me and I do not bleed. Your diversity is bullshit, your sameness empty. I've abdicated all your generosities and naturalised myself to all and everything unmade, unmaking and natureless.

But these are all minimal malformations, your average epochal antagonism, mere oppositional amusement. I don't want to shit in everyone's mouth and then it all be over.

It doesn't matter so long as everyone gives up.

Like what we have.

And all my desired objects at the same speed.

One in each hand and scrutinised, two pigtailed heads in silhouette, and some cartoonish, nondescript figure choking on someone else's puke in my stepfather's basement: a formative experience, if anyone's counting.

Gibberish.

But the next thing is going to be the thing.

The next thing?

The very next thing.

The very next.

Weren't we once these smart, obnoxious art brats? When did this frenzied defeatism happen? SCAD's not going to touch us. When did we become Paul Chan's *Pentasophia (or Le bonheur de vivre dans la catastrophe du monde occidental)?*

BOMB EXCHANGE

I guess it's true what they say, say Gogo and Uta and Gerhard in concert, ex cathedra, our collaborative ethos really is just the sum of our vituperations. And with no need to *no shit* their own shitless outpourings, they pause to generate meaning from the suppressed censure, the creeping obviousness of everything always. The same thought inside each of their heads: "Every sin is the result of a collaboration." And because, so far in and so very weary, they get all their quotes second hand, we have Crane via Theroux – the epigraph of a love affair too painful to repeat.

Out of the befouled air of everyone lighting up at once, someone suggests a decentred exhibition about centralised diversity, calls it an oligopoly of token farts. I forget who.

But it's definitely Gerhard saying: Remember Athens, Documenta 14, that goading motto – "Art unites people" – like a jet of hot piss in our eyes.

And the babble starting over:

Funded by the government to the tune of all the NFTs you can swallow.

A survey of art production after us, post-stab-frenzy, post-first-on-venus, whatever…, will say what?

They joyously performed their estranged familiarity with all things human to reluctant audiences the world over.

So what's Documenta 16 going to be about?

Us. We it. There won't be anything else left.

Quinquennial exhibitions are way too ponderous anyway.

Higher quotient of time than of inspiration.

A gifted toddler will make a subversive film about a history of insufficient funding for the kind of work that toddlers like. It will feature headless cats inside glass vitrines, because the toddler was once scratched by a cat, an aggressive tom with black and brown fur and an 85-degree kink in its tail.

My intestinal networks are inextricable from structures of funding, distribution and, ultimately, power. I won't stop until every bad idea I have is financed to completion.

Join the chorus espousing the cult of being alive, how personal lives are an innocuous enough indulgence before you die – and a necessity afterwards.

How else you gonna live with yourself once you're dead?

Standard à la carte denialism.

Didactic assemblages for senseless play.

With serious faces.

There's a reason orifice-inspired architecture is so pervasive.

…dioramas of absurd geographies sliced open along their perpendicular axes, or were they bodies, or the residues thereof, I forget. Anyway, there were anatomical models of uncertainty and illness, disgorged organs used as instruments for sound baths. If you've never puked an organ, your opinions on most things will never graduate beyond the trivial.

A rich archive of visceral ephemera.

Art as a metonym for wanton idiocy.

I once designed a Wanted poster for Xavier Dupont de Ligonnès as a meta-event, as voodoo, and something about the endangerment of water in absurd formats, or else a leading figure in some Haitian collective tailoring artistic subversion and a legalistic rationale for exclusionary politics to the country's burgeoning black-metal scene. It was destined to become a most salient feature in some circle or other before nobody ever thought of it again, and to no end.

Where do we stand on the coercive dynamics of BDSM parties?

Anywhere the nipples clamps lead us.

In the face of speculative gender norms, everyone must play a part in their own oppression.

Did I ever tell you about Miami's thriving art scene?

Did I ever tell you about my soft-core epiphany watching *The New York Ripper*?

The molestation of Alexandra Delli Colli?

Can't see a duck without…, well you know, to this day.

Perhaps depicting ourselves as transparent acetates of adverse possession is no way to be seen.

The museums won't want us.

I heard they create and reinforce monolithic cultural identities at the expense of diversity and truth.

Inequity is such a cosy horror.

The standout piece saw me savagely murder that little art-loving girl at Pinacoteca Agnelli, Turin. Even now it simultaneously conjures erections and delicate, yet distinctly moist, flatulence.

The inevitable union of right samadhi and unfathomable evil.

As an abstract composition comprising sawdust and high-density foam on a blotchy blue background.

I'm spreading my cheeks for commercial abuse.

The lazy double entendre of so many inconsequent smears mounted on cheap card.

The libidinal is so the baseline of consumerism.

A group of London-based artists, sponsored by the ICA, were to spend four weeks interviewing a never-before-contacted tribe in Papua New Guinea. They took with them only a performative armour. Posed as corporate headhunters. Never came back: something about western insensitivities, certain malapropos phrasings.

Cretin casserole.

Stupid stew.

Uta is watching the abattoir scene at the beginning of *Touki Bouki*. She is crying. And wincing. And smiling. She is too many hands holding cigarettes, too many mouths smoking them, a nervy mitosis, a real-life anatomical blur à la David Altmejd.

Sad fact but… Think of the worst thing. After that there is only quantity and duration.

In the BOMB interview, we'll explain how we once had a profoundly inarticulate feeling. Subtly undermining the logic of the human prosthesis, we'll say how we take a simple dripping sound as a substrate to tell the stories of billions of weird outgrowths from depersonalised land-scapes. If they suggest our augmented reality doesn't correspond to real places, we'll mention how good we feel in hotel corridors, how the sour light represents a hypersaturated consumerist dystopia that is at once entrancing and grotesque. We'll be so portentous as to border on camp.

We'll say how tapping into instability can unlock the fuck-all in your soul.

Can we describe ourselves in the most outlandish terms?

Charismatic shitting.

As animadperversions.

As superemotionalhyperdeath.

As kawaii-coated cryptodadaists infused with giallo tropes.

What if we careen into intelligibility? Become remarkably prescient by accident? Profound, God help us?

We should maintain distraction at all costs.

No one revelatory gaze, no one moment of total absorption or comprehension. Dipping in and out of a central pool of murky refractions, we the soupiest quiddity.

Hint our off-site events will go on forever.

Perhaps the commodification of the self, as expressed through the serrated edge of a browser window, will lean into its own situational absurdity.

Is there anything more profound than scrolling through transparent PNGs wondering if grace itself is transactional?

Perhaps anxiety forms the crux of something far scarier than the slow death behind the eyes of gallerists to the masses.

Should I mention I was once accused of seditious excess following a nose-picking incident inflected by slasher films and a seemingly infinite subtext of cinematic rubrics?

An act of rare tenderness.

You know they're going to ask if immunising oneself against suffering isn't just nihilistic frivolity.

I once did an interview on why I do not do interviews and opened with a quote from Lispector's *Near to the Wild Heart*: "I'm afraid to say it, because the moment I try to speak not only do I fail to express what I feel but what I feel slowly becomes what I say." I wanted to end the interview there, but we went on for another hour, talked myself into a sub-sentient blob.

I find the greatest sincerity in hallucination.

I panic there won't be enough goldfish for all the killers.

Or enough dead women in Tijuana to satisfy my hankering for vasectomies.

The usual evergreen subjects.

Uta looks like she belongs somewhere else. She is crouched in the corner giving the room a house-beautiful-bring-the-war-home vibe.

Oi, pig tits! Basta already! I'm getting the collage wobbles.

Bewildered on the one hand, femme maison dangereux on the other.

Do we admit to chopping off their heads, their hands, breasts even, to setting the beds on fire?

To the torsos via Lucio Fontana?

Admit nothing.

Only the snarled networks of all our going nowhere.

Maybe a splash of influence.

Made of seawater.

Nostalgia is a good way of pretending the past isn't the same country in a different hat.

We should wear our T-shirts with Trbusek's *Rabbit Devouring a Man* printed on the front.

We should practise being glib.

Sometimes I made biro drawings of tenuous figures with black stamens spilling from their mouths that appeared mechanically printed, but were, in fact, painstakingly hand-rendered in cheap, utilitarian ink.

Sometimes the afterlives of time-based works across video, performance and audio are somewhere between narcolepsy and indigestion.

Sometimes I lived in abandoned buildings in Chicago, for Frieze London, for a platform to debut an ambitious new commission on the occasion of random ruined people, otherwise scattered indeterminately in a spatial field, placed inside Lucite cubes.

Sometimes a conflation of Buster Keaton and certain sustainably sourced materials is just a way of cutting your own throat with a cucumber.

Sometimes an artist's research into exploitative bureaucracies is simultaneously decorative and hierophantic, leading to the artist's eventual negation of all mediums.

When I say marginal art movement, I mean fashionistas chasing a cow.

When I say Mikhailov's *Untitled* depicts a naked woman in profile with an enormous hernia protruding from her abdomen, I mean I'm not sure I should be wanking off to poverty-porn.

Your arm movements are pure butoh.

When I say we've been living in the metaverse for longer than anyone can remember, I mean verism is nothing but wiretaps on a film set.

When I say anthropophagic gesture, I mean cosmopolitan nihilism, the vitality of outcasts; I mean the polymorphous free association of destroyed objects rebuilding themselves wrongly, the catastrophist monster-erotic of a delicious improvisation.

Gerhard throws up all over himself as if nothing has happened, as if an artist's formal uncertainty had always looked this way.

So many phantasmagorical discontents launched, acquired and bankrupted.

And just the way we absorb art into our giddy genocide.

Our shrill effluvia, our murder for hire.

Our delirious bang bang against a backdrop of new sociocultural configurations.

What if our art is used against us – like Young Thug and Gunna?

I mean, is it even possible for something to be both ugly and untrue?

What if reimagining the future is no less the retardataire than every other garishly confrontational splurge of creative destruction?

Gogo's platinum prolapse at a new art space in New York's Chelsea Market, through November.

This feeling right now is the next Art Basel Miami.

Push the allocentric agenda.

Off tall buildings.

Or someone's haemorrhoidal resurgences coeval with first Columbine then Sandy Hook.

Semen-spattered microwaves as emblematic of the archetypal heteronormative family.

Would you say your pivotal works are rooted in aesthetic ambivalence, an abundance of bleak apothegms, and an uncanny rejection of emotivity?

I'd say radical transparency around asset ownership is blurred by intuiting the ecstatic dimension of marketing aesthetics and the nightmarish violence implicit in many thousands of prostitute deaths in Guatemala.

I'd say dead-ending in demoralising chaos is the ne plus ultra of art.

Soundscaped as the gentle sloshing of a waterboarded lung.

I'm not sure what the crime is yet.

A maliciously rapturous distillation of horror tropes from the gooey interior of existence.

Like our slightly uncomfortable dissonance is based on actual events.

Like the future's return will arrive in time.

Deus absconditus parallels deep biases in AI technology.

Is that a question?

It's what it means to feel that the complexity of the world is difficult to articulate, that it's somewhere on the edge of meaning, a secondary preoccupation behind the cultural apprehension associated with age-related incontinence.

Apparently, they've all had moments in which they experience how everything is more complicated than they think it is.

They overcome it by contraposing images of diseased female genitalia with discomfiting yet exquisitely orchestrated shots of naked children at 47 Canal, of all places.

To express this doubleness, we literally cut a gallery in half.

We be like nouveau Heizer, void as sculpture kind of thing.

Plastic twine round a dirty extremity to take the pain away.

We play the same video over and over again.

It slowly degrades with each repetition.

It's called generational trauma.

How does an obsequious, braindead blob end up with a secret cache of dead wives? Asking for a friend.

What *about* the sorrier aspects of end-of-life infomercials spiralling into kiddy porn?

And what you call our unconcealed delight at the lurid excesses, the spin-off merch etc., only serves to emblematise our deep distress.

And while we did exploit the commercialised vernacular of helpless art-creatures to communicate our dysphoria and lethargy, we made sure to use intrusive indices like shudder-factor to gauge the eschatological import of the latest gentrified subculture.

You could say our dexterous art practice allows for gonzo interventions authored by a dataset.

Four genderqueer protagonists of fanfare and consternation.

Multimedia artists, based in every city you can think
of, suffering from congenital homesickness, iffy bowels
and buggy eyes.

Our central tensions, whose many iterations pervert
the blithely tortured radicality of pessimist pranksters,
revolve around a melancholic insistence.

Can you mention I have a barnet like a particularly
ornate chandelier, and teary eyes, that I have a heart as
protean as a large hole?

By verbal-visual cues, I mean split tongues akimbo –
upward-facing to express a languorous displeasure.

We refuse to be ensconced in your purely documentary value.

If you trace the trajectories of all subalterns-turned-
monster, you'll see the fashion choices are begging for it.

One can never be too homoerotic when it comes to
the conceptual bridging of different species.

One particularly bacterial critic, based in a one-bed
on London's Cork Street, once accused us of superimpos-
ing our heartfelt emotional states on a cold metal puzzle
of deranged structures. Can you imagine? Said we had
inner urges, that our neurosis was expansive and beguiling. Were we pointedly sacrilegious? Were we hypersen-
sitive vis-à-vis dimensionality? Did our oeuvre consist of
waking hallucinations of animal/human slaughter in a
geographically and temporally disjunctive framework of
artifice and Dada and Afrosurrealism circa the end of
the world? Were we photorealistic from a distance?

We would go to Rag & Bone's bathroom and bedaub the entire assemblage in shit.

Tribeca's surface-level trite goes deep.

As distinct from where exactly?

Moving through the world is just a harrowing display.

Persiflage as camouflage.

I was alone, barricaded in my apartment, labelling every iteration of "don't label me" on obsolete-social-media-network-cum-wannabe-snuff-film VampireFreaks.

The world premier will demonstrate our mastery of radio silence.

That's it. No more questions please.

MORE DANGEROUS
INDECISION

Gerhard bought a Bolex and visited the sites
from *Peeping Tom*. A film about a film about filmmak-
ing, the vague idea masking something vaguer that
never formed into an idea. He made a pest of himself,
twice came close to being arrested, asking every woman
he came across if their name was Helen. Could he decompose behind the gaze, same as Mark, became the
thought. Wasn't the voyeur the exact kind of nothing he
needed to be? He wouldn't need to murder any women;
where would that get him? The death-throe-panic of a
few female faces wasn't the answer he was after. Everyone knew how to fear death; he wanted them to fear life
instead. The sites he found were mostly gone: renovated
to the brink, demolished, built on top of, all Powell's
wrong colours and stylised sets missing. Gerhard has
a drink in The Newman Arms on Rathbone Street in
Fitzrovia, scene of the first murder. He drinks until he is
sick on the bar and the overweight Irish barman throws
him out. He asks a passing Labrador if its name is Helen.
He tries to hug the neck and put a tongue in its ear, but

the owner kicks him away. He crawls down Newman Passage and falls asleep with his head on a bin bag full of used sanitary products. When he wakes up he staggers down the road a short distance and enters an upscale chocolatier, where he demands to be taken upstairs so he can take pornographic pictures of the shop assistant. She threatens to call the police, so he buys some chocolate, and leaves. In front of a block of flats in Brent Cross he offers to pay a little girl if he can pretend to kill her. Just pretend? she asks. Just pretend, he answers. You can be like Dawn Kasper, he says, but she's never heard of her. They pretend together until a woman he takes for her mother starts screaming from a window three floors up. He tries to do the same outside Whitefield school, but the mothers get in the way before he can get started. At what was 5 Melbury Road in Holland Park, Gerhard declares himself homeless. The camera pans across the road to number 8, which has escaped demolition. We see Gerhard knock on the front door for a solid half-hour. No one answers. We are left wondering what he had planned, should someone have opened the door. The view cuts down Melbury Road. Gerhard appears to have lost his mind, and is naked lunging at privet hedges. The film ends in the back garden of number 8. The camera has been placed on the lawn – lower than Ozu, but 50mm. All there is is grass, the odd insect.

Uta was scathing about Jani Leinonen's *The Execution of Ronald McDonald*. What the actual fuck was that? Where was the Sweeney Todd spirit, the farmhouse pies made from actual farmers?

Doxxing shouldn't be a thing. There is no need for private or personal space. Nothing you do is interesting or embarrassing or particular to you. You're human, that should be embarrassment enough. There are no details, no specifics of shame that extend beyond this principal handicap. Hence the call to outlaw all so-called secrets. Whatever unknowns remain are left alone, deserving their status.

Will we ever decide?

Do you think there's nomic vagueness?

The distance between two points can be halved forever.

Is someone coming for us when we're done?

I am laughing. I am saying, haven't you worked it out yet? This will never be done.

You think if I ask real nice, Jon Rafman will film my death?

Gerhard went through a period of making movie erasures. Frame by frame he trawled various classics of cinema excising every human. He could make apocalyptic versions of any masterpiece you like: Great Ions, Tokyo Y, Zen Ka, Vert.

Uta once tried to get the public to leave their bodies to her limited company: AFC (Animal Feed Corporation). She had hundreds of thousands of donor cards printed, whereby the bearer agreed for their corpse to be ground down to provide food for pigs, dogs, cats, etc.

The work should consume them to the exclusion of all else. They must find its meaning, must work it out – only they won't. Asymptotes, they will get ever closer but never arrive. They will disseminate the work because it tortures them and a solution must be found, and why should only some of us suffer when we can all suffer. The entire planet will in short time be engaged in resolving the irresolvable work. Nation states will waver and dissolve into each other, same with races, genders, individuals. There will be only the problem and how to stop thinking about it, how to crack its noumenal code,

Like a magic eye picture that never reveals the hidden 3D image, but the need to see it is so great you spend the rest of your life looking through the image you can see in search for the image you can't.

But what is it? What's the thing? Is it even a thing? What's a riddle to which everyone needs the answer? There are plenty of unsolved questions, and virtually no one cares. Problems in physics, mathematics, philosophy, and even the few that dedicate their lives to solving them are most of them not destroyed in the process, driven mad or whatever. Whatever this thing is, there's no such thing.

Is this a joke? Is the joke that we become the victims of what we want to inflict on others, by not being able to come up with what the fuck it could be? Is this what's happening?

At the Erin Cluley Gallery in Dallas I'm far enough away from New York to feel what abstraction means. The inflight movie was by Bill Viola. Marnie Weber had designed the uniforms like we'd crash landed already. I work within a history of decomposing images in the hope that some of that decomposition will rub off on me. I should stage a more swoony ambiguity. I should trade my sieve for chicken wire, sift my subtleties through that. And if I have to wear an invisible force field, does it have to be quite so unbecoming, so offensive to the buyers who cannot see where their money is going. It's going to take every drop of my princely saliva to swallow this bottleneck. I work on my gestures through some imagined intersection of imaginaries, stressing the indistinct to render unfamiliarity banal. In other words, just how much disinterest will it take for you to love me? My dread comes in all the familiar shapes: dog-shit swirls, bitten toast. Art was an object-orientated force running up against my illusion. The crowds came and went and wrote essays in blood on neon hieroglyphs. I'd sit down to eat but it's all food these days, barely a strand of hair. Faceless is the new face is not what I'm saying. I put words in my mouth before they do, and the result is the same. I spent an entire year desaturating Mondrians and God didn't show up once. The planes were grey and somehow everyone knew this already. I happened on reality and it wasn't profound. Agglutinative languages are a mouthful of nothing. I contrast like with like. I oppose self-portraits on humanitarian grounds. I rely on premeditated whims. My best work is reminiscent of a likeness you won't be able to place. An artist shouldn't have to remind the viewer to see, or to think. If we contain multitudes, we're going to need a bigger bomb. I visited so and so at his studio in Los Angeles, and we were both speechless at how much more there was to say that wasn't worth saying.

To complement my skilfully encoded nonsense I have a serious face. I feel like a lone locust in the gardens of Versailles. If I see another landscape with water

and mountains and grazing deer I'm getting all pissy. I
don't want to have to disambiguate your confusions of
depth, but the legacy of Luminism left me stuck in this
dark hole. By contrast, there's no way into my work but
every possible way out. There are other ways to baptise
a horse, and all of them involve leading it to water. They
say what's the artworld coming to when I can't make
African nail fetishes out my garden shed in Barking? I
confess only to the masterpieces you can see. It's difficult
to say ephemera with your foot on a landmine. I aspire
to virtuosic expressions of universal truth that cannot
quite comprehend the intentionality I assign to them.
The literal meaning of abstraction means equivalences
don't matter. I pull away from a world made impossible by realism. I admit to having slaughterhouses where
other people have sentiments. And when I say other people I mean them, a turn of phrase turned bad. I of the
vertical swipe, of the unmistakable lineage of artificially
contained morphing, of the translucent reflection made
opaque: I is grisaille, faux gestalt of see-through impasto,
vaporous belch of melted cerebellum. I use homage as a
way of shitting back into myself. I would show you my al-
tered light, but I don't know you that way. Out of respect
for an artist's vision, I distract myself with banalities. It's
wonderful to watch jaguars hunt birds. It's wonderful to
remove something from this world. Some people think
cognitive space roughly translates as room to think. My
first encounter with art was an axonometric projection of
every possible world at once. The minutes subsequent to
it became known as my fertile period. Another profound
moment in my life was when I went to Buenos Aires and

went to bed and didn't get up for a month. I didn't know anyone in the city so I started dying; I started to fade out and it all came together. I soon realized every fucker opens their mouth is a raisonneur of some non-existent author. They use their brains like blenders so they get to swallow anything. My accidental death from carbon monoxide poisoning at any age was a wearable solution.

We were dressed in Memling carpets saying how genius is what involuntary systems do. As part of our final exhibition we invite the audience to interpret the work literally. The materiality of my suggestion awakens illusionistic potential in the otherwise unsuspecting. A kaleidoscope of insipid curators-in-residence sing a song to our successful disintegration. I make everything bigger than it needs to be, so I can poke more holes in it. I have to trust that the grand disruption is coming. It's always the same story, always that nagging how about I set you on fire and then see how far your living in the present gets you. Our vestigial figures are saying something about a cleansing experience gone wrong, some somatic altarpiece to our disembodied madness. It's not the end if we can destroy ourselves forever. I grew up in a culture of endless sensuous crevasses I did my best avoid. The explanation desecrates but wtf. Synesthetes be all like the celestial void tastes like dirt, and then what? Cannibal feast somewhere in the Bois de Boulogne? It was spring and her abstract period became our second child. I would paint back then like Roberto Matta, purely retinal stuff, blobs of October, imagining my face was Victor Brauner's plucked eye pic and people could tell. I learnt Jesus was abused as a child. No scented baby wipes. Found

constant references to concrete irrationality in my insom-
niac dream diary. We were related in that we had the
same human father. Even where we came from his name
was Duchamp. He taught us the *beauty of indifference.*
Duchamp went about the dehumanisation of art and
failed: I mean, just look at the state of it now. We were
sent here to finish what he started. The face I see in the
mirror is literally in the mirror; it has nothing to do with
me. More than all the seeing, there is what we came here
to show you. The problem and the solution are the same:
there is nothing to do. It's one of those bromides us artists
eat up. We forgive everything because you have done
nothing; we forgive nothing because of everything else.
We can't stay here, it's fucking horrible. We'll leave behind instructions for others to enact. We've got to go before they catch us, before they analyse us to death.
Problem is humans are useless at pretty much everything.
But they do make good copies of themselves. And the
food's not bad. All this boredom's making me anxious. I'd
had my fill of emptiness years before I decided all it
needed was a good polish. Can you imagine the force of
will it takes to pull out all your teeth with a pair of mole
grips? Shit for brains that I am, it's a case of gagging on
every word. Horror has nothing to do with it: I can pleasure myself with the most monotonous strokes. Of course
it gets away from me at times – times like now. Though I
can always get the better of good feelings, of contentment
and of peace, with a little sassy self-harm. We need to at
least hypostasise our art for as long as it takes. All these
vicissitudinous tangents and recombinative fusions to no
established end. I can barely reach the tips of my fingers.

The sound of necks breaking was muffled by thickening sleet, thought Uta as a way of refusing to confront the suspiciously cancerous growths in her neck. It's considered bad practice, the height of rudeness or whatever, to take much notice of these human maladies. Nobody wants to die a human death, not even humans. Another day and no closer to art forgetting where it came from – in time to arrive someplace. Just say the word and it'll start all over again. I ask you, is this any way to arrange my permutations? It's good to get sick, if you're sick of waiting. The train isn't coming. The train worth waiting for was never coming, unless you built it yourself, with no self to speak of. Imagine a world in which for every prayer you had a snort of laughter instead: different sound, same indefinable pain. They'd only laugh themselves a new religion. Can we just once say what we mean? Exactly how stupid are you? I've been as good as human for years, I'm supposed to keep track? You want a cure for the hearts we don't have. When are we going to turn art into mathematics and be done with it? And poetry into Word Search while we're at it. There is a moment before you start when you really ought to know it's kind of over already. The press for the show will describe our work as a hovering fractal poison full of oblique moments and quasi-shamanic striations, and us as Zurich warmongers. Will they say we exemplify an emerging international cadre of artists whose secret ingredient impedes the formation of secrets? When this is all over, I may take up basket weaving. I'll write an acerbic survey of the artist's life as satirical fidelity. Because it never existed, Gerhard recreates Hotel Broslin's room 7 in a building on Hubert Street and Hudson, where the hotel's neon sign was positioned – the one from which Duane and Belial hang and fall and for the sake of the sequels do not die. For the exterior shots he visits the office building at 80 Franklin Street, Tribeca, and cries abhuman tears over the many failures of reality. I definitely need to make more MoMA-friendly work. All of which means we lack quintessence. Come for the compositional studies in gouache and pencil, stay for the WASPy cis boy lynchings as ritual offering to the god of bad light and sly mise en abymes. I was never meant to, but I feel most comfortable when my inner neo-surrealist makes her entrails visible. We tried to form a preoccupation with urgent social concerns, but our cross-sensory comprehension of geometrically compromised spaceships got in the way. We're elemental like that. So hard to be generically of the moment. I tried to look goofier like my interior was small when it wasn't. The reasons I wanted they don't want. Just the same. Nothing to do but... I'm reverting to diegetic embeddedness to inaugurate the rise of a new cultural vernacular. For real. A reduced size through reduced opacity kind of thing. VR and the metaverse are expressions of humans unwilling to embrace human redundancy. Their anatomical happiness is NURBS already. I published a maltreatise on unpremeditated subjectivity. Our buffer is we credit no one. Well, no one that doesn't deserve it. I once recuperated in Tehran, from C21 correspondences and too much artworld shit, the formalised lighting, manufactured expressions, all kinds of consumables, automatism of populating this parodic reality, you know. Of course I made a big fuck-off joke of myself, like I can't help but side hustle my milieu.

Shit, he said his carnal preference was enthusiastic and I
needed a place to hide. He used contemporary software
suites to parse complex, irregular curvatures in extravagant acts of love as part of the EAT group. It was seren-
dipity how aerodynamic we were. The shared television in
the lobby was near permanent static like nobody seemed
to notice, and like they didn't even know it was a horror
trope. I mean, people sat down and watched the fucking
thing. This peculiar to Tehran you think? We so suffused
with plastic and exhaust fumes we almost human now.
Do we really have to conceive it first? They'll buy anything. But will they buy nothing? What is it we're selling?
Some liturgical act or object, I guess. We need to get more
aggressively asymmetrical, more sprawling, more grandly
installational, more MoMA, more intimately exiled, more
cookie dough for the sweet-tooths, more purposely psychiatric, more starfish skeleton, more decomposed jaguar,
more mercurial metonymies, more CGI inversion, more
mimetically charged stimuli, more jocular riffs, haloed
slapstick, monadic murderlust, idiosyncratic research lab
paranoias, computer-generated intimacies, modular scar-
ring, flattened processes, migratory realities, loosely suggested… Do you still have the preparatory drawings? You
see our awkwardly articulated bodies have kind of a votive
aspect. The way we move kind of precious in its irregular-
ities, kind of buggy; and while I'm clearly privileging aesthetics over utility, like my knee joints I can go both ways.
Last time I was in Germany it was for the Georg Baselitz
retrospective. A young woman accosted him and started
screaming, to which he calmly suggested she suck his
wife's cock. I mean how many Ambien to never wake up,

right? I'm tired of inventing things that already exist. Artists should invent anonymity. The only thing that excites
me now is fatigue. You see my indolence is boundless. It's
the only part of me that might just last forever. The immortality of just never doing anything. The sprawling infinitude of fuck all. I tell myself the sex you don't have is
the best sex. And it's better that way. I'm fluent in silence
and inaction. Everything else is a piss-poor translation of
a suicide note written under mortal duress. I tried on feeling as a way to get closer to the thing supposedly wearing
it. If it worked we were both too bored to notice.

   We always got room service. We're kind of ashamed
how much we eat and drink and then not. Not really. We
throw most of it out the window anyway. My name for
the current state of things in here is changing by the day.
Yesterday it was sunnier than expected, but we only got
as far as dangling our legs out the windows. Uta flushed
her head down the toilet to cool down, and because her
nose felt dirty – and with her nostrils upturned the bog
water could get right in. Now what was it... that thing
the Marquis de Sade would do?

   Art is the meaning of meaninglessness. Who said
that?

   I don't know, just about everyone.

   So what are we saying?

   Something decimated and alive. The rich totality
of a new madness. Drunks on holiday with flammable
breath. The endless holiday of art. The endless work of
being on holiday when there's no such thing as work.

   Obsessions are everything. The rest is maintenance.
Life's a waste of art.

My picture of reality is what squelches.

Yeah right, I've seen you fuck concrete.

In my dreams.

Strung out on art not being good enough.

Art is eating cunt, never getting full.

Sometimes I think no amount of degrees from the Sorbonne will make this go away.

I try to take heroin like a believer, but no.

My eyes are the best there is. But this shared brain is a kind of blindfold. See shit for the trees of shit. Make a show of twitching.

The man I'm in is dead.

Asked a doctor once: that stomach pump thing, you do that for brains? Said there was no point, that I'd only fill it up again. Smiled like have a nice day or else.

Gogo is running round the room with nothing on screaming get this fucking thing off me.

Gerhard's face is a palimpsest of every version of consternation his features can muster. He holds his hands in his hands. He can feel the movies slipping away.

Uta is writing on the entomology of artists:

Artists are small, wingless creatures with an innate craving for metaporphosis; their bodies are strongly compressed and repressed, sometimes heavily scle-rotised (as a defence against boredom), more or less hairy and shiny and exist in all human colours. They are parasitic in both larval and adult stages, suck-ing blood (meaning) from mammals and birds and technology and science and mathematics and any-thing else. The artist larvae are legless almost from the time of waking, because they are always running from something, elongate, eyeless, with fairly sparse but strong convictions and they have biting mouthparts; they are not exclusively parasitic, but sometimes feed on organic matter (a life) which they find mainly in the usual abode, the drum of their hosts (or parents). The free world contained in their otherwise deoxygenated cocoon.

The Order *Artist* is at present divided into an indefinite number of superfamilies, which together comprise indefinitely more families. The number of described schools and movements the world over is no one cares. More than is necessary have been found in the British Isles alone. Nearly all the artists we've heard of are indigenous to planet Earth, and while a few were introduced from elsewhere in recent times they have found it difficult to successfully establish themselves. These very occasional interplanetary immigrants, who cannot flourish or maintain themselves under the conditions prevailing on this planet, are too often excluded from serious critical attention in art magazines and periodicals. It should be noted that such artists in rural settings have generally taken their own lives for want of anything more interesting to do, and have acquired a certain cache among their more favourably situated kin.

Collecting art from these artists means collecting neuroses and discomforts you cannot properly process or explain or sell on in the art market as it is. A working knowledge of their biology, ecology and systematics is therefore to be regarded as advantageous. Where possible, it is always advisable to mitigate their patchy distribution with unfettered access to anywhere in the world.

Every night we inanimate as is the custom. Imperturbable bodies astronomically inclined on the inside, concave and convex, oscillating amid imagistic arrays of undulant and truncated narratives. So many syncopated seizures behind our closed eyes. Cofounders of damp, atonal ambivalence and curiosity, replete with immodest keening and ingenuity. Arguably all visitants hear the call to don wooden Dogon masks to exuberant effect, take their meth aesthetic to a dance party to which they are not invited. We are of Bill Gaddis' vanishing breed, and are made to feel unsafe because of it. Our Havana syndrome happening elsewhere. Our posthuman sublime a blacklighted power plant, a constructed experience, the halls of the Tyrell Corporation on Zug Island, Detroit, our work veering into ideas about indigeneity and invasiveness, derivative or decorative, subtleties lost in reproductions – remember how we thought we'd have this licked in a blink?

Whatever it is, feels like we're getting further away. But then closer because of it. Kind of.

Kind of fucked then.

Kind of no fucking idea where we are.

Geometries of mush.

And the more we think about it the worse it gets.

Always the way.

The more solutions the more insoluble.

All lousy with funnies and futilities becoming their opposites. Then back again. The cunting carousel of it all.

After a fire we are somehow more interesting. We touch each other and we stay there. Our melted hands melt into melted arms and shoulders. Our faces merge.

Our stomachs blend. You could say the work of fire incites a more sustainable violence. An insurrectionary paradise porn, an imaginary tropical resort catastrophizing our too despondent ars poetica. Remember we would remix algorithmic media, or use machine learning to make generative websites, or integrate VR-mediated puppets into edgy flirtations with sexualised war crimes? And we escalated into this, this hair-raising, concurrent decline of impersonal histories and complicit subversion. The smug mockery of our ominous innovations.

I've got to get out of here.

Ugh, all wanderlust is puerile.

Lines of meandering text to amplify a virtually non-existent narrative.

An agitated line with no identifying marks.

I think I must have hit my head. TV looks all parallelepipedal.

Can a thing take place? Are there still prizes? The windows are therapeutic, as if there are opportunities for beauty outside. The interplay of silent documentaries disturb the clumsy waltzes. The way we look so terrible in photographs. A single, exaggerated contradiction, a sexless crochet. This preoccupation with humming our existence, waiting for the words to come. So many elaborate routes to inaction. Can we dance and call it philosophy and not throw up? Can we press a button and continue walking off the edge of all the buildings? Is this a walkthrough September? Will the next toothless head have eyes in its mouth? A kind of dentistry of loss, I guess. There is no need for our experiment to prove anything. We do not plan our bodies' disintegration into code, the intimacy of decay, a new dimensionality a day or so before we die. We have been gummed to death in the snake pit of the photographic instant. The onlooker performs the modalities of any given moment, the clinical manipulations in gigantic detail: slogans of their own hackneyed claustrophobia. My liberal conception of art extends to the smell of my shit versus yours. In our first major exhibition, the audience will be comprised entirely of sick children. They will be asked to be brazenly tragicomic.

We trust the sensationalist media to tell the truth about the world – performatively speaking. An artist writes/performs masterpieces in sign-language, and the translators into English and German go insane.

… the rolling emergence of arson motifs, burn everything to the ground, the depiction of overrepresented emotion claimed as deceptively simple, but nothing deceptive about it, banal weapons entering the blockchain, our predicament seen in less generous light, the surveillance state on us, our hypervisibility, crazed control panels and at the same time the most abstracted of D-based artists. To still be waiting, and all the ways we've tried to make sense, to insufflate our airless lives.

By mid-afternoon, on I forget the day, we watched a feed from the Giardini during Venice Biennale, usual crowd, Arte Programmatica mannequins blurring into one another, Kunsthalle directors pushing themselves to the front, faces like interchangeable horseshit. It had the look of an experiment gone wrong, a transitional installation orientated toward permanence, a bleary-eyed impulse toward spectacular boredom. The art was barely a participatory factor, all of it just crowd, just the functionalism of turning up, just the slow accidental brain death of abject experimentalism they'd all come to expect and love. We sat quite still, the legwork you don't see thickly impastoed, just us trudging through gloopy precincts to arrive at a clearer understanding of our confusion.

We watched an invisible performance, an elaborate troll of our subaltern histories and experiences, slim pockets of unoccupied space whose comb-like armatures evoked perpetual universes of nonbelonging. Uta is in the bathroom with the door open. Gogo is watching her from the bed. She is masturbating with her fist while chewing on a toilet brush. Taken together they look like a strained palindrome for the never-ending end of days.

Ours was an institutional critique. We curated practices rooted in embodied writing. We plucked luminaries from sewers and crack dens and caravan parks and council estates and slums and homeless shelters and red light districts and they all ended the same way: trapezoidal cutouts for trapezoidal holes. Gogo is eating from the ashtray again. They say the pressure on an individual to represent a diverse demographic is too much to bear. I heard it said at Lubov in New York. I subscribe to this truth for want of another in any particular moment. Practitioners whose ultimate goal is to make good art form tentacular congeries of zoomorphic debasement are so much exposed circuitry. They sport their transfiguration of art like flaccid strap-ons. And here we are failing on their terms, our bodies loose bird shit shrouding a windshield. Known for our hyperreal contortions, this reparative bent makes us tear at skeins of wire connected to wall outlets, the disquieting gravity of our blood-cracked eyes, cochineal veins on white ceramic, tinged with years spent dismantling the deliberate malfunctions, or affected anomalies, of a venally operated art world. We see the human rendered in a series of lame-dick clichés and know they will be repeated forever. We have a clinical flair for being as profoundly pointless as possible. Pencil scrawled on diazotype. A modular composition with abstract wearables organised into irregular compounds, menacing details revealed under microscopes, material vocabularies of constraint-based Dada antics, the soft megalomania of our inhuman longings.

I think we gave up on ever going home. We had to destroy the world and we couldn't even manage to destroy ourselves. We turn our faces to the sun and there's a horizon of sorts. An omnivorous ocean behind our eyes. Whatever we do now is proportionate to the degree to which we are inadequate. There is only this mission; we will not be given another. For lack of a better way of saying it, we scream till whoever's upstairs starts banging through the ceiling, and the concierge comes tapping at the door. It is raining outside, so we whisper in a corner by the window and watch the sky's dripwork darken the road. We think no one will hear us if we just never stop talking. To appear less berserk we form a huddle so our heads are touching. Our sentences intersect and overlap and run in and out of each other until we are univocally tentative and forlorn and out of reach.

I remember in the beginning we tried to undo art. From our confusion came nothing, so we went with it, but it didn't work. We unpainted, unsculpted, uninstalled, unperformed, and so on. We created a procession of undoings. Our exhibition, in a disused plastics factory, was made up of empty canvasses, empty plinths, empty display cases, unpeopled performances. The whole thing was underwhelming. These reversals were, quite evidently, the merest pubescent fumblings – a precocious lassitude. And that we culminated in a body of work which wasn't, proved the most indelible tell. It was nothing more than nothing. For the fact it came to an end, that we were finished with it and that it finished (without anything to show for it, without ever getting started), undermined the entire project. Only when we started something that would never be finished, the *impersonified continuum*, would we discover the art we needed to make – be finished with finishing, get the fuck away from these places we'd been forced to inhabit. The revelation arriving at this crestfallen juncture: Our *dangerous indecision* cannot only be danger-ous for us. Everyone capable of experiencing it must be made to – through the art, the art acting as gateway to the precipitous vacillation that lies behind it, inside, and beyond. And we have only to carry on breathing, but in the void of space, but coming back and starting over, but never getting anywhere, but passionately aimless till it hurts to breathe, but breathing anyway, and dying too, breathing and dying and breathing while dead.

And so on and so – introspectively chewed to bits, outwardly dissolving – dreaming we are done with it all, the four of us free our blizzard of flea dirt, techniques to piss away a bored far off gesture, to concoct a mani-fold tease, a grinning misery dish for the spaniel-souled clunks at our disposal.

It is a machine that palpitates and fluctuating between distension and its opposite can be thought to
breathe – a swelling machine, a beautifully ugly dress-up
of a kind of life that lives, because it cannot itself sustain life, via the sucky, indiscriminate fawning of those
whose motivational infrastructure (in stark contrast to
the ossified globules of their identities) is so hazardously
porous, so readily penetrable from without, that their
entire motor system is up for grabs in what averages out
to a few seconds. (The psychopharmacologists will arrive, flounce, take notes, only to inevitably succumb to
the same, to the very condition they attempt to diag-
nose, before ever accessing their preliminary findings.)
Having concluded that a prevalence of unchecked affir-
mation was a scourge of requisite magnitude, but also
hilarious in its own right, we couldn't resist. You come
across a soft spot you can't help but touch it, press down
hard, push your finger in as far as it will go. You see, once
they start applauding they cannot stop. It begins spontaneously and though they all soon think about stopping,
imagining the spontaneity of the end will arrive as im-
pertinently as the beginning, no such conclusion arrives:
they clap and/or nod and smile and soon find there is
nowhere else to go, how these small purposeful actions
are all they have, and how trying too hard to override
the urge only makes the movements faster, more vigor-
ous, eventually painful as their underdeveloped muscles
tire. Our vaunted stimulus lived or survived according to
its pious order. And eventually illimitable zeal runs up
against inadequate reserves of air and strength, arms and
necks lagging wearily for want of water. Cute little video

does the rounds: kids gin the mother through a straw till she too drunk to stand. We discover how devotees increase in direct correlation to the ubiquity of immodest claims to artistic immunity. Just lotsa behaviour and all of it the same: a feedback loop of dissolving rats in our oozy loveglaze, pulsating constellations in clear jelly. We look to reach before the week is out a full complement of pervious types, aka human beings. Because death entails the schedules that precede it, I operate my celebratory fervour by smell. We digress to wonder, Do our cuticles need attention, our hair lopping? Did our thoughts make it happen? Eroded snap joins in their conscious reality forming such funny pathways. And Gogo talks of applying sperm to any one of them at any time, then has a snooze instead. Their dying meaning very little, of course. A motionless dance, a sedimented adieu, fine attitudes dunked in hot tea. If we come on all solemn in the mirror, over a single white basin, perhaps it's the abyss of throttling ourselves in our sleep. Perhaps the grouting in of floaters, when what we wanted was ontological relief. Perhaps phonetic meanderings in vanished grass. Perhaps an almost human failing after all. After all this. After living like we meant it, like we were ever here.